"I think I had better stay," Mike announced

His voice was decisive. "I don't know where else to look for your husband so it seems that's the only way I'm going to catch up with him. And besides, I don't like the idea of you being out here on your own."

Penny stared at him, aghast. "But you can't," she protested. "The caravans are all locked up."

"I wasn't thinking of staying in a caravan," he responded with unruffled calm. "That settee will do me well enough."

Penny felt herself blush. "Sleep in here? But—"

He smiled suddenly, an incredibly attractive smile that transformed his harsh features. "Don't worry, lass," he assured her gently. "You're very pretty, but you're far too tender meat for my taste."

SUSANNE McCARTHY has spent most of her life in London, but after her marriage she and her husband moved to Shropshire. The author is now an enthusiastic advocate of this unspoiled part of England, and although she has set her novels in other locations, Susanne says that the English countryside may feature in many of her books.

Books by Susanne McCarthy

HARLEQUIN PRESENTS

Don't miss any of our special offers. Write to us at the following address for information on our newest releases.

Harlequin Reader Service
P.O. Box 1397, Buffalo, NY 14240
Canadian address: P.O. Box 603,
Fort Erie, Ont. L2A 5X3

SUSANNE McCARTHY

tangled threads

Harlequin Books

TORONTO • NEW YORK • LONDON
AMSTERDAM • PARIS • SYDNEY • HAMBURG
STOCKHOLM • ATHENS • TOKYO • MILAN

Harlequin Presents first edition June 1991
ISBN 0-373-11372-2

Original hardcover edition published in 1990
by Mills & Boon Limited

TANGLED THREADS

CHAPTER ONE

'Oh—QUICK, Lizzie, the phone! You answer it. If it's someone called Mark, tell him Samantha decided to take the job in New York, after all.'

Her friend cast her a jaundiced look. 'Penny Carter! You've been up to your tricks again, haven't you?'

Penny gurgled with laughter. 'Yes,' she confessed blithely. 'But, Lizzie, he was *awful*! Going on about his Porsche and his share options—I couldn't resist teasing him just a little bit.'

'Are you in to Ian or Roger?' Lizzie asked drily.

'Of course.'

Lizzie smiled 'Do you know something? If you weren't my best friend, I'd probably hate your guts. It's just not fair, the way you get them all running after you!' She disappeared into the hall, but a moment later she was back. 'It's all right—it's only your brother.'

Penny's sapphire-blue eyes lit with delight. 'Oh, great!' She bounced out into the hall, and picked up the phone. 'Hi, Pete,' she greeted him cheerfully.

'Penny? Is that you?' His voice sounded unusually agitated.

'Of course it's me. What's the matter?'

'Listen, I need your help, sparrow. Can you

come up for a few weeks?'

She laughed wryly. 'Well, I don't have much else to do. Now that the January sales are over, it's back to the dole queue for me.'

'Good girl. How soon can you get here? Can you come tomorrow?'

'Of course I can.' She frowned, absently picking up a pencil and doodling on the back of an old envelope, as she was prone to do when she was concentrating. Pete had never asked for her help before—never asked for anyone's help. He was her big, dependable elder brother, solid as a rock. 'What's wrong, Pete?'

'I can't really explain over the phone,' he said quickly. 'You won't hitch-hike, will you?'

'Of course not—I never hitch alone. I've got the coach fare.'

'I'll give you the money when I see you But . . . listen, sparrow, I won't be here when you come.'

'Why? Where are you going?'

'It's a bit of a long story, and . . . well, it isn't the sort of thing I can explain over the phone. But that's why I need you to come—to keep an eye on the place while I'm gone, feed the dogs. Look, I'll explain everything when I see you. I might be gone a couple of weeks. I'll leave the key under a brick beside the gate, and some money in a margarine tub in the fridge. And there's plenty of food—you shouldn't have to go down to the village at all. In fact . . . I'd rather you didn't.'

Now Penny was becoming seriously alarmed. It wasn't like Pete to get into any sort of trouble. He was the most sensible, reliable person she had ever known. 'Pete, what is going on?' she questioned urgently.

'I told you, I'll explain it all when I see you. But I don't want you to have to tell anyone who you are. If you *do* see anyone, just . . . fob them off.'

'What if they think I'm a burglar or something?'

He laughed. 'Oh, it won't come to that. No one's likely to come all the way out here—they'd have no reason to. Except . . .' he hesitated, and then added carefully '. . . if a man called Mike Wolfe comes looking for me, I want you to tell him you're my wife.'

'*What*? What on earth for?'

'I told you, I can't explain now. But it's very important.'

Penny hesitated only for a brief second. She knew it must be important—Pete would never ask her to do anything so outlandish otherwise. 'All right,' she agreed. 'Who is he, anyway?'

'You can't mistake him. He's a Geordie, he's thirty-five and he might be driving a truck—a big thirty-eight tonner, bright red. He's built like a truck himself, too. But don't let him bully you, sparrow.'

Her eyes flashed with a belligerent light that would have been a grim warning to the unknown Mike Wolfe, had he been present. 'Don't worry, I won't,' she asserted darkly.

Pete laughed. 'I don't suppose you will! Anyway, he won't take it out on you . . . I wouldn't leave you there if I thought he would.'

'Take *what* out on me? What's going on? It isn't like you to run away from a fight.'

Pete hesitated again, as if debating with himself. 'No, it's better if I don't tell you . . . that way you can't let anything slip by accident. Just remember . . . convince him you're my wife. Promise?'

'Of course I promise,' she assured him, though she was utterly mystified.

'Good girl. Listen, I'll ring you every night, and if there's the slightest hint of trouble it won't take me long to get back to you.'

'I'll be all right,' she insisted. In the tough part of London where she'd grown up, girls learned early to take care of themselves.

'Thanks, sparrow. I really appreciate it. Bye now—see you soon.'

'Goodbye, Pete.' She owed her brother a great deal. She had been only twelve years old when their mother had died, after a long illness, and it had been Pete who had comforted her—their father had just gone to pieces. A few months later he had suffered a fatal stroke—but Penny had always believed he had died of a broken heart.

The Welfare had suggested she ought to go to a foster home. But Pete wouldn't hear of it. There weren't many young men of twenty-one who would have given up so much of their own freedom to make sure a kid sister had a proper home. Penny knew that it was mainly because of her that he had never got married—he'd had plenty of girlfriends, but none of them had been too keen on having a troublesome adolescent always hanging around.

And now he was in some sort of trouble; there was really no question that she would do anything she could to help him. But what on earth was it all about? And what did it have to do with a bullying truck-driver called Mike Wolfe?

'Ouch! You look as if you're planning a murder. Not me, I hope?' Ken, who lived in the flat upstairs, had sneaked up close behind her and wrapped his arms around her waist.

She smiled up at him. 'Oh, I don't *think* it'll come to that.' she responded, a gurgle of laughter in her voice.

He reached over her shoulder and picked up the envelope which she had been drawing on. 'Hey, that's very good,' he approved. 'What is it?'

'It's Moriarty, of course,' she retorted, snatching back the sketch of the landlady's cat that he was deliberately holding upside down.

He nuzzled into the soft dark curls that tumbled around her shoulders. 'Mmm—your hair smells fabulous,' he murmured. 'What are you doing tonight? Fancy a hot curry and some cool music up in my penthouse?'

She laughed at his description of his dingy attic bedsit, but shook her head. 'Sorry, I've got to get up early tomorrow—I'm going up to stay with my brother for a couple of weeks.'

'I'll give you a lift to the coach station,' he offered.

'Would you? Oh, thanks, Ken.'

'That way you can spend more time in bed with me in the morning,' he added hopefully.

'Oh, no.' She moved her arms sharply, releasing herself from his grasp. 'I've told you before, I'm not going to bed with you.'

'Why not?' he asked, with all the arrogance of a young man who knew how good-looking he was.

'I like to be unique,' she retorted crisply, her large eyes dancing.

He laughed. 'I don't believe you. There's no such thing as a twenty-year old virgin, not these days.'

He caught her again, and after a playful tussle claimed her mouth in a kiss that was indeed very tempting. It was only the sound of a door opening downstairs that broke them apart.

'Damn—the Dragon!' muttered Ken, letting her go. 'Come on, Pen, come upstairs.'

'No,' she whispered firmly, retreating as their nosy landlady began to plod slowly up the stairs. 'Goodnight, Ken.'

'Goodnight,' he conceded reluctantly. 'Give me a call in the morning, and I'll take you to the coach station anyway.'

She smiled warmly. 'Thanks, Ken. You're a good egg.'

'I must be losing my touch!' he sighed, rolling his eyes.

The wind was howling like a banshee off the Irish Sea. Penny lay in bed, listening to the eerie sound. It was so isolated out here—spooky, almost. She'd been here barely twelve hours, and already the solitary confinement was driving her crazy.

She had thought it would be quite nice to get the chance to relax for a while, after the hectic pressure of the West End store where she had had a temporary job for the Christmas rush and the sales. But she missed the bustle and noise of London, the banter of her friends in the big old house in Camberwell where she and Lizzie shared one tiny bedsit.

How could Pete stand it out here, month after month, all on his own? But of course he wasn't here from choice. Poor Pete—he really hadn't had the luck he deserved. He'd just been made up to shift-manager at the factory where he'd worked since leaving school—the youngest shift-manager they'd ever had—when the place had suddenly been closed down, without warning.

Jobs were hard to find, so he and some of his mates had put all their redundancy money into starting up on their own. It had been a tremendous struggle—he'd worked so hard—but they'd just been too small to compete. They'd gone bankrupt, and lost everything.

He'd hated being unemployed, but the only job he could get was as odd-job man and winter caretaker on a caravan site out here on the wild coast of mid-Wales. He lived in this tiny two-room cottage with his dogs—all saved from a premature dispatch by the RSPCA.

He'd been here over a year now. At first he hadn't been very keen on letting Penny stay behind in London, but he had reluctantly had to concede that she couldn't go with him. And though she had been only nineteen then, he had had to admit that she'd had her head screwed on.

For about the fiftieth time she found herself pondering Pete's mysterious behaviour. He had rung her last night, but he had been as evasive

as on the previous day. At least there had been
no sign of this Mike Wolfe—but it was early yet.
Would he come today? Pete had been sure that
it was safe for her to be there on her own, but she
was still a little apprehensive.

And why was she supposed to make the man
believe she was Pete's wife? Maybe he had
thought that a married man would seem more
respectable? Less likely to disappear altogether,
perhaps, if he'd left a wife behind? Was that
it—was her presence supposed to allay suspicion,
give him a few days' start on his adversary?

'And what do you lot know about it all?' she
enquired of her furry companions. There were
four of them now: Prince, a not very bright
mongrel; Goldie, who undoubtedly had some
Labrador in her parentage; Butch, a
disreputable-looking Jack Russell; and a little
newcomer, aptly named Rags—a bundle of soft
black fur that had kept her feet warm all night.

They jumped up as she spoke to them, wagging
their tails eagerly. But whatever they knew, they
weren't saying—they were far more interested in
coaxing her out of bed to take them for a
walk.'OK, OK, I'm coming,' she conceded wryly,
swinging her feet to the floor.

At least it was warm inside the cottage—Pete
had left the wood-stove in the other room burning
for her. Pulling off her thick cotton nightie, she
had a quick wash, and dressed in her jeans and
a soft pink jumper she had knitted herself, and
then padded through into the living-room, the
dogs at her heels.

The cottage was over a mile from the nearest

village. It was very small—just this one room, with the tiny bedroom behind it, and a lean-to bathroom tacked on as an afterthought. The furniture was old, but well cared for, and Pete kept it very neat, the big table in the middle of the room polished and gleaming, the brasses that hung beside the fireplace shining like mirrors.

She made herself some breakfast, and then took the dogs out for a walk along the beach. She had been up here in the summer for a cheap holiday. It had been a pleasant spot then. The caravan site was in a sheltered cove with a fine sandy beach—perfect for family holidays. But now it was mid-February, and the sea was a stormy grey, whipped by the wind.

It was a relief to get back to the cottage. She turned on the television, just to hear the sound of human voices, made herself a cup of tea, and then settled down in the armchair with her book. But before long the antics of the dogs had distracted her, and she couldn't resist finding a pencil and some paper and capturing them with a few swift sketches.

She had always enjoyed drawing—if there had been the money, she would have loved to have been able to go to art college. But it was a waste of time pining for what could never be . . .

She was thoroughly absorbed in her doodling when her canine models suddenly leapt up, ears cocked, tails lashing aggressively. She jumped up and ran to the window. A huge red truck was negotiating the narrow lane. It was travelling fast, grunting irritably as the driver swung it hard round the bends, menacing the hedges.

With a hiss of powerful air-brakes it drew up beside the cottage. She stepped back quickly from the window, her heart pounding. So he'd come—Mike Wolfe. What was she going to do now? Her first instinct was to hide, but he had probably seen her at the window. And anyway, Pete had said it would be all right.

There was a moment of tense silence, heavy in contrast to the noise the truck had made, and then there was a crashing knock on the door that seemed to shake the whole cottage, and a string of loud profanities that would have made a docker blush.

'Carter? Open this door, you bastard, or I'll break it down!'

It seemed that he was on the verge of doing just that. 'Wait!' she called, her voice rising to a squeak. She pulled back the bolt and jerked the door open, her face white. 'Go away!' she gasped. 'He isn't here.'

He was about eight feet high and three feet wide, and he breathed fire over her as he barged past her into the cottage. He ignored both her and the dogs as he strode purposefully across the room, snatching open the bedroom door, and then on to search the bathroom.

She stared after him, her nerves shaken. The dogs were barking vociferously at the bedroom door, but none of them seemed willing to actually confront the intruder. 'A fat lot of good you are,' she muttered at them crossly. What on earth was she going to do?

It was all very well for Pete—wherever he was—to assure her that Mike Wolfe wouldn't take it out on her. On first impression, he seemed like some kind of psychopathic maniac! She looked around wildly for something to protect herself with. The bread-knife was on the table, and she snatched it up impulsively. As he came back into the room she turned swiftly, concealing the blade behind her back.

'Where's Carter?' he demanded. His voice was as rough as industrial sandpaper, and he didn't sound as if he'd had much practice in keeping his temper.

But she certainly wasn't going to let him bully her—who did he think he was, marching in here like this? She squared her shoulders, and glared back at him defiantly. 'He isn't here.'

He made an impatient gesture with his hand. 'I can see that,' he barked. 'Where is he?'

'I don't know,' she insisted firmly.

'When will he be back?'

'I don't know that, either.' She injected several degrees of frost into her voice. 'Now will you please go?'

He shook his head. 'No way, lass,' he responded implacably. 'I'm staying right here until that bast . . . until Carter gets back. I don't care if I have to wait a week.'

She drew herself up to her full five feet two. 'I told you to go,' she repeated, her voice taut with suppressed panic. What was she going to do if he refused? Her fingers tensed around the reassuring handle of the knife.

He looked down at her, a very threatening Goliath menacing a small but indomitable David. A puzzled frown creased his brow. 'And who are you?' he demanded bluntly.

He took a pace towards her, and she retreated, only to find the table at her back. 'I said get out,' she hissed, bringing the knife round and holding it in front of her in a purposeful grasp.

He looked surprised, and then to her amazement he burst out laughing. He had a strangely pleasant laugh, husky-edged, like his voice. 'Nay, then, lass,' he chided, as if reproving a recalcitrant child, 'put that down.'

Her eyes flashed at the mocking note in his voice—as soon as she had done it, she had realised that it had been an absurdly melodramatic gesture. But now she didn't know how to back down without increasing the danger of this bizarre situation.

And then, with a movement that was startlingly swift for a man of his size, he caught her wrist, jerking it upwards and prising the knife effortlessly from her numb fingers. She found herself curved backwards across the table, imprisoned by his hard-muscled body.

'I told you to put it down,' he taunted her, a glint of amusement lighting those deep hazel eyes, just inches above her own. 'You'd have neither the strength nor the nerve to use it.'

Penny's heart cartwheeled alarmingly. The physical encounter had been sudden and unexpected, leaving her breathless. She stared up at him, her heart racing.

He was big, though not as big as her fear had perceived him—probably only a little above six feet, but ruggedly built, with an impressive breadth of shoulder. His face was rough-carved, but oddly handsome—and he was more man than she had ever encountered. The woman in her responded instinctively, before her mind could grasp what was happening and get it under control. Their eyes exchanged the primitive message.

He stepped back, looking at her as if seeing her properly for the first time. His eyes took in a slim figure, and a decidedly pretty face crowned with a mass of dark curls. 'Who *are* you?' he repeated, a note of interest in his voice.

Her brain had gone numb, but she answered automatically, 'I . . . I'm Penny Carter.'

A spark of renewed anger flared to life in his eyes. '*What*?' he roared. 'You're his *wife*?'

Only then did she remember the part that Pete had wanted her to play. She nodded dumbly.

'God Almighty,' he muttered under his breath, and sat down heavily at the table.

She stared at him, her mind in turmoil. He seemed quite taken aback by the information that she was Pete's wife. But why? And what on earth had the two of them quarrelled about? It must have been something quite serious to bring him here in this murderous rage.

She studied him cautiously. He was wearing hard-wearing jeans, and a heavy leather jacket with a sheepskin lining. His hair was brown, cut very short to suppress a slight tendency to curl, and she guessed that he was about in his middle thirties.

He looked up at her, and she sensed the effort it was costing him to leash his anger. 'Look, lass,' he said, those hazel eyes searching her face, 'I'm sorry I scared you. But are you sure you have no idea where your husband is? I really need to see him. If you know, please tell me.'

He spoke with an urgency that she found hard to resist. It was fortunate that Pete had refused to tell her where he was going, she reflected—she had a feeling that this man could be very persuasive when he wanted to be. His voice was deep and rather pleasant, the Geordie brogue adding a lilt that was absolutely fascinating.

She forced herself to meet that penetrating gaze. 'I . . . I'm sorry,' she responded as evenly as she could. 'He left this morning—he said he might be gone a couple of weeks.'

His eyes narrowed with shrewd suspicion. 'Does he do this kind of thing often?' he persisted.

She shrugged her slim shoulders. 'Now and then,' she responded, trying for a note of casual unconcern.

He raised an enquiring eyebrow. 'And he leaves you out here in the middle of nowhere all on your own?'

Her mouth felt dry—it wasn't easy to lie to him. 'Oh, I don't mind,' she asserted with some attempt at a smile. 'I've got the dogs for company.'

He laughed sardonically. 'And for protection?' he enquired, casting a sceptical glance at the four of them, who were now fawning at his feet, eager to make friends.

She laughed too. 'There's loyalty for you! But I don't need protection—no one ever comes out here.'

'I came,' he pointed out, the glint in his eyes reminding her of that fleeting moment of physical contact between them.

'Yes ... well ...' She could feel herself *blushing*!

He regarded her for a moment in silence, and then stood up. 'I think I *had* better stay,' he announced decisively. 'I don't know where else to look for you husband, so it seems as though that's going to be the only way I'm going to catch up with him. And besides, I don't like the idea of you being out here on your own, even if he doesn't give a damn.'

She stared at him, aghast. 'But ... You can't!' she protested. 'The caravans are all locked up. And besides ...' She gazed around helplessly.

'I wasn't thinking of staying in one of the caravans,' he responded with unruffled calm. 'That settee will do me well enough.'

She felt the colour in her cheeks deepen to a hot scarlet. 'Sleep in here? But ...'

He smiled suddenly, an incredibly attractive smile that transformed his harsh features. 'Don't worry, lass—I'm not going to pounce on you,' he assured her gently. 'You're very pretty, but you're far too tender meat for my taste.' He strolled towards the door. 'Now, be a good girl and make me some coffee,' he added. 'I've driven all the way from Dover without a break, and I've got a powerful thirst.'

She bridled with indignation. 'I suppose you'd like me to cook you some lunch, too?' she retorted tartly.

He glanced back over his shoulder, a provocative glint in his hazel eyes. 'Good thinking, canny lass,' he approved mockingly. 'Just a snack will do—beans on toast, with a couple of eggs sunny-side-up. And maybe some sausages if you've got them.'

'You call that "just a snack"?' she protested, her voice wavering.

He laughed, and patted his lean stomach. 'Ah, there's a lot of me to feed.'

'I can see that,' she returned without thinking.

He slanted her a look of ripe meaning that left her suddenly tongue-tied. She turned away quickly, her heart pounding, and made herself concentrate all her attention on filling the kettle.

'Hey.' She met his eyes reluctantly. 'You don't have to be afraid of me,' he said softly. 'You're quite safe—I'm no cradle-snatcher.'

'And I'm no baby,' she countered—and then immediately regretted her impulsive words.

He let his gaze slide over her assessingly, admiring the slender curves in the clinging pink jumper and tight jeans. 'Aren't you?' he taunted. 'If you're out of your teens, I'll eat my hat.'

'Well, I hope it goes down well with beans on toast,' she retorted with spirit, 'because I'm twenty-three years old and I've been married for five years!' After all, if she was going to lie, she might as well do it in style.

But his reaction wasn't quite what she had expected. He stopped smiling, and that dark glint of anger was back in his eyes. 'Is that so?' he enquired, a chilling note in his voice. 'You must have been very young when you married.'

She swallowed hard. 'I was eighteen,' she confirmed, reminding herself to be careful what she said. It was essential that she kept the details of her story consistent—he would certainly notice any slip she made.

His mouth hardened into a taut line, and he nodded briefly. 'I see,' he murmured, half to himself. He went out, shutting the door firmly behind him.

Penny drew a deep breath, consciously trying to ease the tension in her spine. A few moments later she heard him reversing the truck round into the lee of the cottage, its warning horn bleeping like an alien space-ship. She stared blankly out of the window as the red monster slid by.

None of it made any sense—except perhaps Pete's hurried departure. No sensible man would stay around to reason with the likes of Mike Wolfe—he was the sort who would use his fists first, and ask questions afterwards. And though her brother was no wimp, he was no match for the powerfully built truck-driver. She could only hope that he would be able to find some way of sorting out this mess—he couldn't go on running forever.

And meanwhile, Mike was going to stay. A memory swirled into her brain, so vivid that it almost took her breath away—of how it had felt to be so close to him when he had taken the knife off her . . . of that husky laughter, that unexpectedly attractive smile . . .

An odd little shimmer of heat ran through her. Though he had said she was too young for him, he wasn't as indifferent to her as he had pretended to be—she had seen that look in men's eyes too often to be mistaken.

And he was going to stay the night here—not just tonight, but every night until Pete returned.

And Pete had said he could be gone a couple of weeks!

Surely he wouldn't really stay that long? Apart from anything else, he had a thirty-eight-ton truck outside, and someone was going to want it back.

But for a while he was going to stay . . . She caught herself up sharply. Heavens above, was she going *crazy*? He'd barged his way in here, shouting and swearing, using threatening behaviour—he was nothing but an ignorant bully! He drove his truck too fast, too. He was just a big, beefy truck-driver, and not her type at all.

CHAPTER TWO

ALL the time Penny was cooking his meal she was on edge, still shaken by the impact of the past few minutes on her emotions. It was impossible now to believe that just a short time ago the cottage had felt empty and lonely. His presence seemed to fill it.

He wasn't watching her—he was sitting at the long table, idly tracing the checks on the tablecloth with the tip of the bread-knife, his thoughts abstracted. But she was totally aware of him, aware of the aura of sheer masculine power that he seemed to radiate quite unconsciously.

She managed to find everything without having to hunt around—that could have aroused his suspicion that she wasn't as familiar with the layout of the cottage as she ought to be. She piled his food on to a huge plate, and set in down in front of him.

He glanced up, smiling briefly. 'Thanks, lass. That looks great.'

She couldn't quite stop herself smiling in response, but she turned away at once and went to fetch the coffee. She didn't bother to ask him if he took sugar—she just brought the bowl to the table. If he way anything like Pete, he'd take about half a dozen spoonfuls.

'Is that all you're having?' he asked, casting a

disparaging glance at the cheese and pickle sandwich she had made for herself. 'No wonder you're such a little sparrow.'

His words brought an unexpected little glow of pleasure—Pete had often called her that, in a joking, brotherly way, but when this big man said it, somehow it seemed to imply . . . fragile, delicate . . . She caught herself up on a thud of alarm— what was she thinking? The last thing she needed was to let herself be attracted to Mike Wolfe. She was going to need all her wits about her if she was going to carry off the deception she had begun.

She watched him covertly from beneath her lashes as he tucked into the gargantuan meal. He ate quickly, with appetite, but there was nothing to complain of in his table manners. And his hands were beautiful—big hands, built for work, with strong, straight fingers. But the nails were cut very short, and there wasn't a trace of dirt or oil around them.

'What did you want to see Pete about?' she heard herself asking.

His eyes came up, and focused on her face, and she felt herself blushing a little under his intense scrutiny. 'You'd better ask him that,' he ground out. 'It's not for me to tell you.' He studied her long and hard, and she shifted uncomfortably, feeling trapped by his gaze. 'What did your parents think of you getting married so young?' he asked.

'Oh . . .' She shrugged her shoulders. 'They . . . they died a long time ago.' She hadn't intended to tell him that, but it would be better to stick as close to the truth as possible. And the tinge of sadness in her voice wasn't feigned.

'I'm sorry.' He sounded it, too, and those hazel eyes held a glow of sympathy. How could such a brutish man have so much sensitivity? 'How old were you?'

'Twelve. My mum had leukaemia, and then my dad died a couple of months later—I think he just didn't want to go on without her.'

'So what happened to you?'

'Oh, I . . . went to live with a relative—a cousin.'

'Were you happy?'

She stared at him. Why all these probing questions? 'Yes, I was happy,' she asserted firmly.

He nodded, as if filing away her answers. 'What about money?'

Her eyes narrowed. 'What do you mean?' she asked warily.

'Your parents must have left you some security? A house? Insurance?'

'What are you? The Gestapo?' she demanded defensively.

He smiled, but the smile didn't reach his eyes. 'I'm sorry,' he said, with little trace of apology. 'I just don't see much evidence of it.' He glanced pointedly around the small cottage.

'Well, there wasn't any money,' she threw at him. 'The house was owned by the council, and there was only just enough insurance money to pay for their funerals. I know what you're getting at,' she went on furiously. Her anger made it easy to lie to him. 'You think Pete married me for money, but you're wrong. He isn't like that.'

'Isn't he?'

'No, he is not!'

He shrugged his wide shoulders in cool indifference. 'Well, I dare say you know him better than I do,' he drawled, a note of hateful cynicism in his voice. He pushed his chair back from the table, and rose to his feet. 'I'm going for a walk,' he announced abruptly. 'I've got some thinking to do.'

He hooked his jacket up from the back of his chair, and strolled towards the door. At once the dogs were with him, their tails wagging optimistically. 'Stop it!' Penny scolded them. 'Sit.'

'Oh, they can come with me,' he offered, stroking Prince's head.

She shrugged dismissively, and turned her attention to clearing away the debris of their meal.

He was gone for a long time. For a while she occupied herself with tidying up the tiny cottage, then she made herself a cup of tea, and sat down in front of the wood-stove to watch the television again. There wasn't much on—a test match from India, a soap opera, a programme for toddlers. She turned it off impatiently, and went to fetch her book. But she couldn't settle to that, either.

Where had Mike got to? Surely he hadn't got lost? He didn't seem the type—and, besides, he'd got the dogs with him. Anyway, it was time to start cooking the dinner. What would he fancy? Maybe it was going a bit far to think about grilling a steak. He hadn't said what time he would be expecting to eat. Maybe a casserole, then—with dumplings.

And a dessert—he'd like a dessert. Apple pie, with nice, thick, creamy custard.

Cooking for him again? a niggling voice taunted inside her brain. We are getting domesticated aren't we? So what? she argued with herself. She'd always enjoyed cooking. She'd taken on the job when her mother had first become ill, but lately she had had little chance to indulge her skills—in the tiny bedsit she shared with Lizzie, the kitchen was no more than a couple of cupboards, a rickety old fridge, and a very old electric cooker with only two rings and an oven just big enough for a medium-sized chicken.

She was happily up to her elbows in pastry-making when the telephone buzzed. She bit her lip. It would be Pete again. What would he say if she told him Mike Wolfe was staying? He'd probably come racing back—and she wouldn't care to witness the ensuing confrontation! No, better not to tell him anything, not yet. Give him time to bring whatever plans he had in mind to fruition.

She brushed her hands down, and picked up the receiver. 'Hello?' she answered breezily.

'Penny? How's it going?'

'Fine.'

'Not feeling too lonely?'

She laughed, careful to inject just the right amount of buoyancy into her voice. 'Not at all—it's nice to get a bit of peace and quiet after all the rush of the sales.'

'Good. Any sign of Wolfe yet?'

'He showed up this morning—steamed through

the place like a bat out of hell.'

'But he's not still hanging around?'

'Of course not,' she assured him in her most innocent voice.

'Good. Be careful, though—he might come back.'

'Don't worry, I'll be all right. Anyway, I've got the dogs here to protect me,' she reminded him, tongue in cheek.

He laughed drily, as if he knew exactly how much use they'd be. 'Of course! Well, cheerio then, sparrow—thanks for everything. Look after yourself—I'll ring you tomorrow night.'

'OK. Bye, Pete.' But the pips had already gone, and she put the receiver down and stood staring at it for a moment. Now she had lied to Pete. It had been for his own protection, of course . . . Or was she lying to herself? Did she want Mike to stay around a little longer?

Quickly she shook that thought from her brain. Of course she didn't want him to stay—except . . . it *was* a little eerie out here, especially at night. It would be nice to have someone else around.

But where *was* he? It was gone six o'clock, and pitch dark. What if he'd had an accident? The rocks were pretty treacherous around here—or maybe he'd gone down on to the beach and got caught by the in-rushing tide? Maybe he wasn't coming back . . . But no, his truck was still parked outside.

It was stupid to worry, but she couldn't help it. On an impulse, she turned the heat down under the vegetables, picked up her duffle-coat and hurried outside. Which way would he have gone?

Instinctively her footsteps turned towards the steep path down to the beach.

The night was bitterly cold, and the wind whipped her voice away as she called his name. She cupped her hands to her mouth. 'Mike?' But there was no reply. As she got nearer, she could see that the tide was out, and the dogs were romping on the beach. But there was no sign of Mike.

Suddenly she was really worried. She ran down the path, calling frantically. 'Mike—where are you?'

A hand touched her shoulder, and she whirled round—catching her foot on a loose rock, and losing her balance. He caught her quickly, and for a brief moment she found herself held close in those strong arms, her cheek against the hard wall of his chest as he set her on her feet.

Her heart skidded, and began to race out of control. Once again she was overpoweringly aware of that compelling aura of masculinity, and the hectic response it awoke inside her. Those deep hazel eyes were looking down into hers, and for one wild moment she almost thought . . . that he was going to kiss her.

But quite abruptly he let her go. 'Where's the fire?' he enquired, a sardonic inflection in his voice.

She drew in a sharp breath. 'Oh . . . I . . . dinner's ready, and I . . . wondered where you'd got to,' she gasped, hoping he would think her flushed colour was due to her hurry.

'Well, let's go, then,' he suggested drily. 'We don't want it to get cold, do we?' He whistled, and

the dogs came bounding up. She smiled wryly at
their obedience to his summons . . . it had taken
her ages to get them to come back to her when
they had been enjoying themselves.

It flustered her to have him watching her as she
served up the meal. Had that moment down on
the path been only in her imagination? It had been
over so quickly, and yet . . . *Careful*, she reminded
herself sternly. Keep your distance—you mustn't
let this get out of control.

He ate with the same single-minded concen-
tration as he had devoted to his lunch—*two*
portions of apple pie—and then he sat back with
a sigh of contentment. 'Mmm. That was good,' he
commented approvingly. 'You really know how
to look after a man.'

She felt a faint blush of pleasure rise to her
cheeks. 'It's nice to cook for someone who
appreciates it,' she murmured, thinking of her
flatmate Lizzie and her endless diets.

He lifted a quizzical eyebrow. 'Oh? Carter's
tastes must be at fault,' he commented drily.

Damn—she had almost slipped up again. 'Oh,
I didn't mean . . . Of course Pete enjoys my
cooking,' she amended quickly. 'But it's different,
isn't it? I cook for him every day.'

His expression was sceptical, but he responded
only with a bland, 'Of course.'

She could feel her colour rising, and stood up
quickly, 'I'd better wash up,' she muttered,
avoiding his eyes. She ran a bowl of hot water,
and turned to collect the plates from the table.

He stood up, and, to her surprise, he began folding up the tablecloth.

'You wash, I'll wipe,' he offered.

'Thank you.' She was emboldened to slant him a cheeky smile. 'Your wife's got you well trained,' she added audaciously.

His eyes glinted with sardonic amusement. 'I haven't got a wife,' he informed her drily.

'Oh . . . Ow!' The washing-up water was scalding hot. Tears of pain stung her eyes.

Mike moved her gently aside. 'You go and sit down, lass,' he said. 'I'll finish up here.'

She blinked up at him in astonishment—she hadn't expected to find such a considerate side to his nature. Her feelings were in turmoil—it was as if she had been riding an emotional roller-coaster all day, and suddenly she felt very tired.

She curled up in one of the armchairs in front of the stove, watching the flames flicker behind the thick glass doors. She wasn't sure how much more of this she could stand. Mike Wolfe affected her more than any man she'd ever met.

It was ridiculous. They had nothing in common—he was a truck-driver, some fifteen years older than her. And even though he had conceded that she was pretty, he had made it clear that she wasn't his type. He probably went for women of his own age, who knew the score, who *really* knew how to please a man . . .

'Penny?'

Her eyes flew open, and she jerked up in her seat, almost knocking over the cup of coffee he was holding out to her. 'Oh . . . sorry . . . thanks,' she flustered breathlessly.

He smiled, and sat down on the settee, stretching his long legs out in front of him. His big feet were encased in boots of soft, well-polished tan leather. As she studied them surreptitiously from beneath her lashes, it slowly dawned on her that they were the sort of very expensive, hand-made boots that were sold in the small shops in Bond Street, just round the corner from the West End store she had been working in.

The rest of his clothes, too, though casual in style, were of the best quality. He obviously made a lot of money driving his truck. She remembered that he'd said he'd just come up from Dover; he probably did mostly long-haul work to Europe and beyond—she'd always heard that that was well-paid. Well, that was something safe for them to talk about, at least. But just as she was about to ask him about it, he cut abruptly across her thoughts.

'How did you know my name?'

She stared at him blankly. 'What? I . . . Well, you told me,' she protested, trying for an air of innocence.

'No, I didn't.' That shrewdly perceptive gaze was searching her face, and she could see suspicion in his eyes.

She bit her lip. 'Pete told me,' she confessed in a small voice.

'What else did he tell you?'

'Just . . . that you might come. That's all.' She lifted her eyes to meet his. 'He didn't tell me why.'

A flicker of wry humour crossed his face. 'That

doesn't surprise me.'

'What has he done?' she asked him, leaning forward earnestly. 'Please, tell me.'

He shook his head, his mouth set in a hard, uncompromising line.

She hesitated. 'Couldn't you . . . If you could just talk to him calmly, I'm sure he could explain. I'm sure you could sort something out.'

'I'm not interested in his explanations,' he rapped, giving her a glimpse of that boiling anger that seethed just below the controlled surface. 'When I get my hands on him——'

'You won't hurt him?' she protested in horror.

The shadow of a frown darkened his brow. 'You must love him a hell of a lot,' he mused.

'Of course I do!'

'There's no 'of course' about it,' he argued. 'Love and marriage don't necessarily go together.'

Confusion held Penny speechless. For a moment she had quite forgotten her role, and now she couldn't remember if she'd made any serious gaffes.

Those hazel eyes regarded her with a steady gaze that was almost hypnotic. 'You don't have to go on pretending that everything's perfect in your marriage,' he said softly.

Panic was rising inside her—in her attraction for this man she was almost letting him lure her into betraying her brother. 'What would you know about it?' she threw at him in heated defiance. 'You just told me that you're not even married. Of course we've had our ups and downs—all couples do.'

He laughed cynically. 'All that loyalty! I

wonder if Carter knows what a damned fool he is?' he murmured.

Suddenly she knew that she couldn't stay in that room another minute. 'I . . . I think I'll go to bed,' she stammered. 'I know it's early yet, but . . . it must be the sea-air. I'm so tired.'

She stood up quickly, but he rose too, and she found herself once again dangerously close to him. She stared up at him, her heartbeat racing out of control. Some strange spell seemed to have spun itself around her, and as he put up his hand to her cheek her lips parted, warm with the anticipation of his kiss.

His thumb moved, and gently brushed away a tear that had spilled over without her knowing. 'Goodnight, Penny,' he murmured, that husky-edged voice very soft.

As his hand fell, the spell broke. 'G . . . goodnight,' she gasped, and bolted like a rabbit for the seclusion of the bedroom, slamming the door behind her and leaning against it, closing her eyes.

She felt shaken, stunned by the unexpected impact of her own reactions to him. He could stir feelings inside her that she had never experienced before—feelings she didn't know how to handle. A sudden image came into her mind, an image so vivid that it took her breath away—an image of herself being swept up in those strong arms, her struggles subdued with kisses.

Resolutely she thrust the disturbing vision away. Somehow she was going to have to find out how to control her own wayward desires—and fast. Although he had so far kept his promise not to 'pounce', he was too much of a man not to respond if she seemed to be offering him an invitation.

It was quite warm in the bedroom—the fireplace in the living-room backed on to it, so it shared the heat from the wood-stove—but the bathroom was very cold. She had a quick wash, and scrambled into her nightie—Victorian white cotton and broderie anglaise, very virginal, as Ken had teased her on one occasion when he had seen it among her washing at the local launderette.

She had made herself a hot-water bottle earlier, and it was nice to snuggle down between the warm sheets. But sleep wouldn't come—however hard she tried, she couldn't forget that Mike was in the next room. So close . . . And yet, for some reason, she was quite sure that he wouldn't come in.

Instinct told her that he would never want to be accused of taking advantage of her—he had too much pride. And, besides, she was sure that he wasn't exactly starved of female company—there would be plenty of women who would be more than willing to appease an appetite that probably matched his appetite for food.

She opened her eyes, and lay staring up at the shadowy ceiling, trying to rationalise her own response to him. He was good-looking—there was no denying that. But compared to some of her boyfriends in London—Ken, for instance . . . She tried to conjure those handsome features in her mind, but the image had faded.

Maybe it was just a natural feminine reaction to the circumstances—finding herself cooped up in the middle of nowhere with him like this . . . But it was more than that. Mike Wolfe exuded a sure masculinity that would make women weak in any circumstances.

A prickle of apprehension ran down her spine. It would be dangerous to indulge any more foolish fantasies about him—because if he should ever decide to overstep the invisible boundary he had drawn for himself, he wouldn't be content with just a few kisses . . .

And she was supposed to be a married woman. She owed it to Pete to keep her promise, to go on convincing Mike that she was his wife, no matter what. Already he had asked a lot of probing questions. She couldn't afford to arouse his suspicions further.

And yet it was strangely comforting to know that he was there, in the next room. She remembered with a trace of surprise how chillingly alone she had felt last night. Somehow it seemed impossible now to imagine a time when Mike Wolfe hadn't been around—a large, rather unnerving presence, filling her whole life.

She woke early, and slipped out of bed, pulling on her duffle-coat over her nightie. Then she crept over to the door. Mike's quiet, regular breathing told her he was still asleep. She stood for a moment listening to the sound.

How long was he going to stay? Surely not for the whole two weeks until Pete came back? She

would never be able to keep up the
pretence—already she had forgotten half the lies
she had told him.

Rags had slept on the bottom of her bed again,
though the others had stayed in the sitting-room
with Mike. Now the little dog yawned awake,
paused to scratch one flopping ear, and then
jumped down on to the floor to ask politely to be
allowed out.

'All right,' she whispered softly. 'But
quiet—don't wake Mike.'

But inevitably, as soon as she opened the door,
the other three dogs stirred, and came bounding
towards her excitedly. As she tried anxiously to
hush them, Mike woke, and unwound himself
from the blanket he had slept in, sitting up with
a yawn.

His brown hair was tousled with sleep, and his
jaw dark with a day's growth of beard. One of
those slow, compelling smiles unfurled as he saw
her standing nervously, half-way across the room.
'Good morning,' he greeted her, his manner
faintly teasing.

'Good morning,' she responded with as much
dignity as she could muster, feeling rather foolish
and inelegant with the hem of her nightie
drooping beneath the scruffy old duffle-coat. 'Did
you . . . did you sleep all right?'

'Yes, thank you. Did you?'

'Very well,' she responded, hoping he wouldn't
notice the betraying shadows under her eyes. She
went over and opened the front door to let the
dogs out.

To her surprise it had snowed during the

night—not heavily, but just enough to carpet the ground with white and gild every branch of the trees that screened the caravan site from view. The dogs raced out into it excitedly, skidding and rolling, digging intently as if convinced there were frost-bitten travellers buried beneath.

Mike came over to stand beside her. 'Mmm—quite a nip in the air,' he remarked. 'No one's going to be moving far in this.'

'No, I suppose not,' she agreed—which meant that, even if he had changed his mind about waiting for Pete, he would have to stay, at least for today. She hugged her duffle-coat around her body, leaning back against the door-frame so that she could look up at him properly. He had taken off his sweater, and was wearing a faded denim shirt, the top button undone to reveal a smattering of dark hair that curled at the base of his throat.

She stared at it, utterly fascinated. There was a strange intimacy in being so close to him like this, both still rumpled from sleep. It was almost as if . . . they had spent the night together. What would it have been like, to be held in those strong arms, to feel the heat of that powerful male body against hers . . .?

He was watching her, a glint of interest in his eyes as if he could read all the thoughts in her mind. Her mouth felt suddenly dry, and quite unconsciously she ran the tip of her tongue over her lips. Something flamed in the depths of those hazel eyes, and he put up his hand to coil one finger idly into a dark curl that lay against her cheek.

The temptation to run her fingertips along the rasping line of his jaw was impossible to resist. He smiled as she touched him, and leaned towards her, his mouth brushing lightly over hers—light as in a dream. A shiver of heat ran through her. She had wanted this to happen, from the moment he had stormed into the cottage yesterday morning.

He drew back, but of their own volition her hands caught at the front of his shirt, pulling him to her, her lips parting to invite his kiss. His mouth closed over hers, and his tongue swept deep into her mouth, swirling languorously over the sensitive membranes to plunder every secret corner.

His arms had wrapped around her slender waist, beneath the duffle-coat, and the heat of his body through the thin cotton of her nightie seared her soft skin. He was lifting her almost off her feet, curving her against him so hard that her head swam dizzily. She had been kissed many times, but never like this. This was out of control, a mutual hunger that would be setting off fire-alarms all down the coast.

At long last he lifted his head, and smiled down at her, a gleam of sardonic amusement lurking in the depths of his hazel eyes. 'Well, good morning,' he murmured, as if slightly bemused by what had happened.

Reality swung back with a stunning blow. Her cheeks flamed scarlet, and she stepped back quickly, hugging the duffle-coat around herself, acutely conscious that her flimsy nightie had concealed little of the contours of her body.

'Don't!' she gasped.

He quirked one dark eyebrow in quizzical amusement. 'Don't what?'

'Don't . . . don't touch me.'

He laughed mockingly. 'Well, now, lass, it seems to me that you were the one who began it.'

'No, I didn't!'

A flicker of anger lit his eyes, and his smile hardened. He turned away from her, shrugging his wide shoulders in a gesture of indifference. 'Suit yourself,' he drawled. 'I'm a little too old for kids games. And you're not using me to soothe your bruised ego—if your marriage is on the rocks, that's your problem.'

A stab of horror almost took her breath away. She was supposed to be posing as Pete's wife—not letting herself be kissed by his mortal enemy! She drew a deep, steadying breath, holding herself aloof. 'Well, I . . . I suppose you're expecting me to cook breakfast for you now?' she threw at him challengingly.

'I'm not expecting anything, lass,' he countered, his words embracing a multiplicity of meanings. 'But if you'd like to do it, that would be fine.'

She stared at him for a moment, struggling to restore the rational part of her mind. 'Right. I . . . Well, I'll go and get dressed first,' she stammered. 'Then you can use the bathroom after me.'

She escaped quickly to the bedroom, closing the door behind her. This was crazy—what had got into her? Though she had tried to deny it, she knew that he had been right—she had been the one who had started it. Something drew her to him, like a moth to a flame.

She moved over to the chest of drawers, and stared at her reflection in the mirror. Those big sapphire-blue eyes, that usually brought her so many facile compliments, seemed to mock at her. Ever since she was fourteen she had been able to wind the boys around her little finger. But she had never had the least difficulty in keeping things under control.

She had always thought she was smart—smarter than some of her friends, who fell so blindly in love, giving the lads everything on the strength of a careless promise, getting themselves a bad name, getting themselves pregnant. She shook her head wryly. 'You're not so smart,' she told the image in the mirror. 'You just never met a man like that before. And the first time you do, you're like putty in his hands!'

Maybe it served her right—sometimes, she had to admit, she'd probably been rather cruel to the young men who were so eager to flirt with her. She hadn't intended to be—it had been just thoughtlessness. Well, now she knew how it felt to burn for someone who seemed able to cool off at will.

With a small sigh, she picked up her hairbrush and tugged it through her thick, dark curls. Maybe it was just as well that Mike was able to exercise a little restraint. She didn't seem able to—and that could lead to all sorts of complications.

CHAPTER THREE

'IT DOESN'T seem to be thawing yet.'

Mike glanced up from the book he was reading. Penny could sense the frustration in him. She could guess what he was thinking—although the snow wasn't deep, it was enough to make these narrow country roads treacherous. He would know that Pete wouldn't be back for at least a few days. And he was the type of man who would find it difficult to tamely wait.

'It isn't very heavy,' she added, a slightly uneven note in her voice. 'Maybe this'll be the last of it. It might thaw tomorrow.' The atmosphere between them had been awkward all morning, neither of them speaking much. Every time Penny thought about what had happened, she could feel her cheeks tinge with pink—and it seemed that she was thinking about it all the time. 'Would you ... would you like some lunch?' she offered awkwardly.

He turned his eyes to her, as if his thoughts had been miles away, and then one of those slow smiles unfurled, turning her knees to jelly. 'Good thinking, canny lass.'

'I ... I could do you another fry-up?' she managed brightly.

'Sounds good.'

'Right.'

She got out the frying-pan, and set it on the stove, glad to have something to do. But after a moment he came over to watch. 'Mmm—smells good.' He leaned past her, and plucked a mushroom from the hot fat, popping it into his mouth with savour.

It was unnerving to have him so close—it made her clumsy with the spatula, chasing the fried eggs round and round the pan trying to scoop them on to the plate. He laughed, a deep, throaty chuckle that made her even worse.

'Well, don't just stand there making fun of me,' she protested. 'Make yourself useful—lay the table or something.'

'OK—where are the knives and forks?'

'In the drawer!' she told him with womanly exasperation.

It was a relief that the atmosphere had eased. Over lunch they chatted about nothing much, and afterwards they found a game of Scrabble to keep them occupied. Penny kept the scores on the back of an old envelope, doodling all around it with sketches of the dogs.

A little to her surprise, Mike was very good at the game, spotting words that she would never have thought of, and he beat her by thirty points. 'That was fun,' she declared, sweeping up the letters. 'Shall we have another game? I have to get my revenge.'

His hazel eyes danced with laughter. 'If you can,' he taunted.

'Don't be too sure of yourself,' she advised, slanting him a mischievous glance from beneath her lashes.

'Maybe I think I've good reason to be.'

Somehow . . . Maybe she was just imagining it, but the gist of the conversation seemed to have shifted, as if they weren't talking about a game of Scrabble at all. It was almost as if . . . he was flirting with her. A delicious little thrill of excitement fluttered through her, try as she might to warn herself not to be so foolish.

It was his turn to begin, and as he placed his four letters he gave her one of those slow, provocative smiles. He had made the word 'BODY'. She swallowed hard, feeling the betraying blush creep up over her cheeks, and quickly fixed her attention on making a word herself. The only thing she could think of was 'DOT', which gave her a paltry four points to open her score.

He took his turn, then she took another. A few turns later someone added an 'S' to the end of 'DOT'—and then again Mike added a word that made her blush: he had spelled 'KISS'. Across the table, she could feel his eyes resting on her, though she couldn't quite bring herself to meet his gaze. A small smile hovered at the corners of her mouth as she put down some letters of her own: 'MAN'.

The board filled slowly. As the afternoon ticked away, Penny was becoming more and more conscious of the fact that they were snowed up here together, isolated. And somehow she was losing her grip on all those good resolutions she had made. There was something quite intoxicating in this little by-play of flirtation.

Of course, he was only indulging her, within the

bounds he had set himself. What was it he had said? He was too old for kids' games. He wasn't taking this seriously, and he didn't intend that she should, either. Besides, it was ridiculous—how could anyone turn a straightforward game of Scrabble into a kind of seduction?

He was watching her across the table, and suddenly he laughed—a low, husky laugh that touched a chord of response deep inside her. 'You know, I didn't think girls could do that any more,' he remarked softly.

She stared at him, bewildered. 'D-do what?'

'Blush like that.' There were fires burning deep in his eyes, and as she watched, held in his strange enchantment, he laid two letters, transforming the innocuous word 'CARE' into the infinitely evocative 'CARESS'.

Her mouth went dry. 'Er . . . that's . . . let me see . . . One point each for the two 'S's—oh, one of them scores double, so that's three, plus . . . six for using the "CARE" again . . .' She took a deep, steadying breath, struggling to concentrate on her adding up. 'You're winning again,' she told him, her smile a little overbright.

He reached over and took the envelope from her to scan the scores. A smile of amusement quirked his mouth as he studied her doodled sketches of the dogs. 'Hey, these are really good,' he complimented her warmly. 'How did you learn to draw like this?'

She shrugged her slim shoulders in a casual gesture, though inside she felt really pleased. 'Oh, I've always scribbled.'

'Scribbled? But these are really clever. I love the way you've given them all such a character—they're almost human! This is the sort of thing that they put on greetings cards and things like that. You ought to try sending some of them off to one of the companies—you might be able to get something published.'

'Oh, no.' She shook her head modestly. 'I've never thought of trying that.'

'Well, you should,' he insisted. 'You've got a real talent.'

He turned the envelope over to see if there were any other sketches on the back of it. Too late, Penny realised that it was addressed to her in London. Instinctively she reached out to snatch it back, but her agitation betrayed her. He looked again to see what she was trying to hide, and then looked up at her, a question in his eyes.

She sat back, deep colour flooding her cheeks. It had been inevitable that her lies would catch her out, sooner or later. But as he handed the envelope back to her, she realised that it was addressed in the modern form 'Ms' instead of 'Miss'—a form that kept the secret of her marital status.

'So you've been living apart,' he said quietly—and it was a statement, not a question.

She hesitated, racked with guilt. This was the moment to tell him the truth—but to do that would be to betray Pete. So she nodded.

'Why did you come back?'

'He . . . he said he needed my help,' she stumbled—it would be best to try to stick as close as she could to the truth. 'He said he had to go away for a few days, and would I keep an eye on the place, mind the dogs.'

She couldn't meet his eyes, afraid to see the anger. But when at last he spoke, his voice was surprisingly gentle. 'Why do you let him do this to you?' he questioned softly.

She stared up at him, her numbed brain unable to find any sort of answer. 'I . . . I . . .' She stood up, retreating from him in self-defence. 'I'd better start the dinner. Would you like shepherd's pie?' Her voice sounded strange to her own ears, and she realised that she was close to hysteria. That gentleness had almost been too much for her—she had wanted only to fall into his arms and blurt out the whole story.

There was a long moment of silence, fraught with tension. Then he stood up abruptly. 'That'll be fine,' he said. 'I have to go and check the truck.'

He picked up his jacket and went out. A moment later she heard the engine of the truck revving up. Her heart plummeted. He was going then—without so much as a goodbye. Maybe it was for the best. If he stayed, it was going to get harder and harder to keep her wayward heart under control.

But even as she blinked back the foolish tears, she realised that he wasn't going. He had left all his things here—his bag was still on the floor beside the settee.. Vaguely she remembered that someone had once told her that a diesel engine needed to be turned over regularly in cold weather to stop it freezing up.

Doubts and questions were spinning in her

brain. Maybe she should have told him the truth, after all. She had an uncomfortable feeling that she had missed her last opportunity to explain the thing properly. If he found out now—*when* he found out—he was going to be furious. She shivered, remembering that stormy anger.

The door opened with a rush of cold air, and Mike came in, cursing and sucking his fingers. 'I've cut my damn hand,' he complained impatiently.

Penny jumped up. 'Oh . . . quick, run it under the cold tap,' she suggested anxiously.

He had sliced rather badly across his fingers, and the cuts were welling blood. 'It looks worse than it is,' he assured her. 'It isn't deep.' He smiled down into her misted eyes. 'It was my own stupid fault,' he added wryly. 'I wasn't concentrating.'

She felt as if her heart had stopped beating. Was he saying that it was thinking of *her* that had distracted him? No—this was getting silly. She turned to the sink, and began to run the cold water over his hand.

'I suppose I'd better put some plasters on them, to keep the dirt out,' he mused, examining the wounds.

'Oh . . . yes, of course.' She looked around in panic, wondering where on earth Pete kept the first-aid box. He slanted her a sardonic smile, and she blushed foolishly as she realised that she didn't need to pretend now—that part of the lie, at least, had been eliminated. He wouldn't be expecting her to know where everything was. 'I'll try and find them,' she murmured sheepishly.

It didn't take long to find them—Pete had a

first-aid kit in the drawer of the dresser. She spilled the plasters on to the draining-board, and selected the ones she wanted. 'Has the bleeding stopped?' she asked.

'I think I'll live.'

He held out his hand, and she patted it carefully dry. The cuts had closed, but they had sliced at a sharp angle, leaving flaps of skin that would collect dirt. She bent her head over her task, carefully wrapping a plaster around each finger, trying not to be too aware of his closeness, but she was remembering all too vividly the way that big, masculine hand had gently stroked the tear from her cheek. And she could feel herself growing warm with the longing to have him touch her like that again.

She finished dressing the cuts, but she still held his hand in hers—and he made no attempt to draw it away. Time itself seemed to be suspended. Fate, having tangled up the threads of their lives, now stood by and watched like some Olympian mischief-maker, waiting to see how they would write the next chapter of their story.

The irrational part of her mind had taken control. She lifted his hand to her lips, and laid one trembling kiss in his palm. Still he didn't draw his hand away, and slowly she lifted her eyes to meet his. He brushed his fingers gently against her cheek, as if fascinated by the smooth texture of her skin.

Her heart was fluttering like the wings of a moth, flying too close to the flame—far too close, melting into a searing hunger that she had never felt before. His mouth closed over hers, parting her lips in hungry demand, and she felt the languorous sweep of his tongue over the delicate inner membranes as he tasted the sweetness of her mouth.

She had longed for him to kiss her again, longed to feel the warm strength of his arms around her, curving her against him, and she responded totally to his insistent embrace, her willing surrender only serving to increase his urgency. His hand moved to brush over the ripe, aching swell of her breast, and he eased her back against the sink-unit, his body hard against hers, making her vividly aware of the warning tension of male arousal in him.

But, as if both sensing at the same moment that they were on a path to danger, they drew apart, gazing into each other's eyes, their breathing ragged. Then he let her go, and drew away from her. 'I'm sorry, lass,' he rasped. 'That wasn't meant to happen.'

She stared at him, memory flooding back. She had told him so many lies, lies that stood between them now as a barrier that seemed insurmountable. Tears rose to her eyes, and with a low groan he drew her back into his arms, cradling her head against his shoulder.

'Hush then, bonny lass. Don't cry,' he murmured. 'There's no reason for you to feel bad about it. Believe me, the bastard isn't worth it.'

She struggled out of his arms torn apart by guilt. This man—this stranger—had almost tempted her into betraying Pete's trust. 'Yes, he is,' she insisted fiercely. 'What would you know about it? You don't know what he's like. He's gentle and kind, and he took care of me when there wasn't anybody else.'

'Penny!'

He reached out to catch her, but she twisted away from him. 'Don't you touch me!' she spat at him. 'Leave me alone. I hate you!' She ran into the bedroom and slammed the door shut, leaning against it heavily, tears streaming down her cheeks.

There was no lock, not even a bolt. He probably wouldn't try to come in, but she couldn't be sure. Quickly she grabbed a chair, and shoved it up under the handle to jam the door. Then she sat down weakly on the bed, and closed her eyes.

How could she possibly be in love with him? He was a rough, bullying truck-driver, with a chauvinistic attitude to women and a casual approach to relationships. She tried to conjure up the image of Ken, of some of her other boyfriends, but that part of her life seemed like a distant memory, like something that had happened to someone else. Mike Wolfe was the only thing that seemed real in her life.

She sank on to the bed, weakly letting herself surrender to the temptation to relive that kiss. She felt again his arms around her, his lips on hers. The pillow was a poor substitute for his solid, hard-muscled body, but at least it was safe to hug it and whisper all the things she wanted to say to him.

When at last she emerged from the bedroom, Mike was sitting in the armchair, watching the cricket on the television. He glanced up as she came in, but he didn't say anything. She crossed to the kitchen end of the room and began getting the dinner ready.

She cooked a big shepherd's pie for dinner. Mike's eyes lit with pleasure when he saw it, and she couldn't suppress a smile. 'Don't you ever get tired of eating?' she asked him.

He shook his head. 'I've a big appetite.' He ate with relish, clearing his plate and looking around for dessert. She'd made a rhubarb crumble, with thick, creamy custard, and he ate two large portions of that before he finally declared himself satisfied.

'Aren't you afraid you'll get fat?' she asked him as she cleared away the plates.

'Not me. I keep myself fit——'

They both spun round, startled, as the telephone buzzed. Penny darted across the room, but Mike was there first. But when he picked up the receiver, he handed it to her. She took a deep, steadying breath, leaning back against the wall as he loomed over her, every line of his body a threat.

'H . . . hello?'

'Penny? Is anything wrong?'

She forced a laugh. 'No, of course not,' she insisted quickly. 'Just . . . It's so quiet here—the ring of the telephone made me jump, that's all.'

'Oh—yes, it does get a bit quiet there. How's everything? No more sign of Wolfe?'

'No,' she lied, gazing up into Mike Wolfe's hazel eyes. 'He was here yesterday, mad as a wet hen, but I haven't seen him since.' For an instant a glimmer of amusement lit Mike's grim expression, but the hard line of his mouth made Penny shiver.

'Well, just watch your step,' Pete reminded her innocently. 'I doubt if he's really given up—he's as obstinate as they come, and he's got a reputation for getting his own way.'

'Hadn't you better come back and protect me then?' she asked, trying to keep that airy lightness in her voice.

Pete laughed. 'Oh, you'll be all right,' he assured her. 'He may look like the original Neanderthal man, but he isn't dangerous. He just might appear again suddenly and catch you out, so be careful.'

Mike's eyes narrowed with suspicion at those last few words. In a sudden surge of panic, she said quickly, 'OK, Pete. Bye.'

'Goodbye, sparrow. Mind——

Mike snatched the phone out of her hand. 'Carter? You get your **** back here or I'll——'

He looked at Penny sharply, and she looked down guiltily at her finger on the button that had disconnected the call. She had barely been aware of the instinctive reaction that had made her do it—and she really wasn't sure why, either. There was more to it than just protecting Pete from Mike's anger. She had a feeling that, once she found out what was at the root of their quarrel, she wasn't going to like it.

But now his anger had turned on her. She tried to side-step away from him, but he caught her shoulders in a fierce grip and pushed her back against the wall. 'You little bitch!' he snarled at her between his teeth. 'What are you playing at?'

Fear and guilt and weakness turned to defensive anger, and her eyes flashed blue fire as she spat back, 'Take your hands off me, you bully! I'm not afraid of you.'

'Well, you should be,' he warned darkly. 'If I find out you're mixed up in this, I'll break every bone in your body.'

'Oh, yes, you're very brave, aren't you?' she sneered. 'Threatening a defenceless girl. You wouldn't be so clever if Pete were here.'

'But he isn't here, is he?' he reminded her in a voice that chilled her blood. 'He's run away—leaving you behind to distract me, like a Judas goat.' He let his eyes wander down over the slender curves of her body in a way that made her quake with apprehension. 'Well, if you're willing to let him sacrifice you to the Neanderthal man . . .'

His fingers tangled in her hair, dragging her head back painfully, and his lips crushed hers apart with none of the gentleness she had known in him before. This kiss was a ruthless invasion. She tried to struggle, kicking and punching him, but he ignored the blows as if they were no more than the touch of a summer breeze.

He was letting his hand rove insolently over her body, savouring every curve, and against her will she felt herself responding, though she knew she was letting him lure her along a path that could only lead to disaster. His hand had pushed up beneath her woollen sweater, sliding up to mould the firm swell of her breast, hiding in the lacy cup of her bra, claiming an intimacy she hadn't the strength to refuse.

Her body melted against his hard length as she breathed the evocative male muskiness of his skin. She was surrendering totally, the last shreds of sanity gone. Now his kiss was neither gentle nor cruel—it took her into another dimension entirely, a world of flagrant sensuality. His mouth moved over hers, enticing, inciting, and with unhurried ease his languorous tongue sought the soft inner sweetness, plundering deep into every secret corner.

But suddenly he drew back, shaking his head, a sneering smile curling his hard mouth. 'Oh, no,' he grated harshly, 'I'm not going to fall for that one.' His eyes slid over her in undisguised contempt. 'You're no better than a whore!' he lashed her. 'Pretending to be so in love with your husband, and yet you can't wait to lie on your back for me, can you? What are you trying to do—get even with him for running off with someone else? Well, you're not going to use me for that.' He turned away from her abruptly. 'These dogs had better have a walk,' he said, and without another word he took his jacket off the hook and strode out into the night.

She stared at the closed door, suddenly aware of a trembling weakness in her knees. She moved over quickly to sit down in one of the armchairs, struggling to regain control of her ragged breathing. His insults had stung, but not as much as the words he had inadvertently let slip. Pete had run off with 'someone else'.

So that was what it was all about—a woman. Pete had stolen away with Mike Wolfe's woman. She should have guessed—that raw anger . . . He must care about her a hell of a lot. Who was she? Not his wife—he wasn't married. And, besides, Pete would never do a thing like that, have an affair with a married woman.

His girlfriend, then. What was she like? She'd be nearer his age—thirtyish, probably. And beautiful—the sort of beauty that came with confidence and maturity. She closed her eyes, trying to visualise. Blonde hair, not too long, and smart clothes—and a pore-deep sexuality that could hold a man like Mike Wolfe for years.

Why had she left him? After all, though Penny knew a lot of women had found Pete attractive, he wasn't in the same league as Mike. Maybe she had got fed up with him being away so much of the time, travelling the roads of Europe and beyond in that big truck. It probably wasn't much of a life, constantly waiting for him to come home.

Or maybe it was because he balked at getting married. Maybe she had run off with Pete as a way of bringing him to heel. Would the tactic succeed? He wasn't the sort of man who would appreciate being blackmailed—but if he loved her, he wouldn't let her go without a fight.

Tears of humiliation stung the back of her eyes. What a fool, she had been, letting herself fall in love with him, letting herself imagine that he was attracted to her. He had accused her of trying to use him to get even, but that was exactly what *he* had been doing. And what sweet revenge, to seduce the woman he believed to be Pete's wife.

It was a good job she had found out, before things had gone any further. It would have been the biggest mistake of her life to go to bed with him—because to him it would have been no more than a casual encounter, to assuage a passing appetite. To her, it would have been everything.

And afterwards, it would have been impossible to remain on Pete's side in the quarrel between the two of them. All her instincts, she knew, would bind her to the man she had fallen in love with, whether he was right or wrong. And she owed a deep debt of loyalty to her brother.

Her eyes fixed on the telephone. Pete would ring again tomorrow night—and Mike would be sure to answer it. Once Pete knew he was there with her, he would come home—and the woman would come with him. And then it would all be over—Mike would talk to her, win her back.

But if the phone didn't ring . . . Pete would probably just think the line was down because of the snow. He wouldn't worry unduly. He'd stay wherever he was—and maybe the longer he had with his mystery woman, the greater the chance that their affair would flourish, and she would choose instead to stay with him.

On an impulse she moved across to the phone, and followed the wire down to the socket in the wall. Damn—it was the old-fashioned sort, not one with a plug that she could 'accidentally' pull out. But maybe that was just as well—if Mike noticed it, he might just plug it back in.

Quickly she searched in the drawer of the dresser, and found a sharp pair of scissors. The wire ran round the skirting-board, behind the dresser. She reached her hand down behind it as far as it would go, and snipped. The wire fell slack.

With a guilty glance towards the door, she arranged the loose wire as naturally as possible, and dropped the scissors back into the drawer. Then she stood back to admire her handiwork. Yes, it was quite dark in that corner—Mike was unlikely to notice what she had done.

CHAPTER FOUR

PENNY woke very early the next morning, and lay staring up at the shadowy ceiling. It had been very late when Mike had come in last night—she had already gone to bed. It wasn't going to be easy to face him today, not after what had happened last night.

After a while she heard him moving around in the next room, so reluctantly she got up, dressed quickly, and opened the door. On the threshold she paused, her heart accelerating alarmingly at the sight of him. He was standing at the kitchen sink, shaving, and he was wearing only those lean-fitting jeans. Her mouth went suddenly dry as she gazed at that hard-muscled body—the urge to reach out and touch the smooth, weathered skin was almost too much for her.

He turned, drying his face on a navy-blue towel, and greeted her with a cool, 'Good morning.'

'Hello,' she managed, struggling to tear her eyes from that broad male chest, to still the longing to play her fingertips through the rough dark hair scattered from his throat to the thick leather belt of his jeans. 'Has it . . . has it snowed any more?'

He shook his head. 'But it's not going to thaw yet—there was a heavy frost overnight.'

'Oh.' She turned away, fixing her attention on

the wood-stove. The ash needed to be emptied,
and more wood brought in from the pile outside.

'I'll do that,' he offered, coming up behind her
as she knelt to draw out the ash-pan. 'You'll ruin
your hands.'

'No, it's all right . . .'

He put his hand under her elbow, lifting her
to her feet. 'I said I'll do it,' he repeated firmly.
'But you can do something for me. I've no clean
shirts—I'd really appreciate it if you'd wash a
couple for me.'

The touch of his hand had sent a jolt of
electricity through her, and she couldn't quite
meet his eyes. 'Oh . . . yes, of course. I'll . . . do
the breakfast first, shall I?'

'Thank you.'

It might be winter outside, but inside it was
hotter than the tropics when she was this close
to him. She moved away, trying to hide the faint
blush of her cheeks from him. He reached out
and caught her wrist, turning her to face him.

'Listen, I'm sorry about last night,' he said, that
gravelly voice softened a little. 'I lost my temper.
But please, lass, if you *do* know where they've
gone . . .'

She shook her head, a heavy pain in her heart.
There was such a look in those deep hazel
eyes . . . He really must love that woman. 'I'm
sorry,' she murmured. 'I honestly don't know.'

For a long moment he searched her face, and
then with a sigh he let her go. 'OK,' he conceded.
'I believe you.'

That made it even worse—sooner or later he
was going to find out the truth, and then he was

really going to hate her. She turned away, busying herself with cooking the breakfast. But she felt as if she were a walking zombie, all the joy of life drained out of her.

It was ridiculous, she told herself over and over. She had known him only two days, he was about fifteen years older than her and not her type at all, and he was in love with someone else. But nothing she could say made any difference—he had turned her whole life upside-down, and even if he left right now and she never saw him again she could never forget him.

It seemed to be a very long day. Penny did his laundry, and a few bits of her own. They dried fairly quickly on the wooden airing-rail above the wood-stove, and then she ironed them, deriving a secret, stolen pleasure from doing such a wifely task for him.

She tried hard not to watch him as he sat in the armchair watching the test-match, but again and again her eyes were drawn to him by a force that was stronger than gravity itself. She noticed the little things—the small scars on his knuckles that could have been earned in street-fights, the way he lounged comfortably in the armchair with one foot propped up against the side of the stove—those details that would always be part of her memory of him.

They didn't speak much—he seemed to have withdrawn into himself, and though he seemed absorbed in the cricket she sensed that he was only passing the time as he waited for the phone to ring. Her eyes wandered guiltily to the dark corner where she had cut the wire. He hadn't noticed.

And as the day wore on, she began to regret her hasty action. Maybe it would have been better to let things come to a head, to force Pete and the woman to return and have it out with Mike. Maybe she would still choose Pete—at least then Mike would know where he stood, and would not have to endure this agony of waiting.

And if she chose Mike—well, it would be better for Pete that it should happen sooner, rather than later, when his attachment to her would have been all the stronger, and the wrench of losing her so much the greater. Oh, if only she hadn't cut that wire!

Where would they have gone, in the middle of winter? Not far, Pete had said. But most places along the coast would be bleak in winter. To a town, then—but which one? As casually as she could, she glanced along the bookshelves for a road-map.

There was only a member's handbook from one of the motoring organisations, and she drew it out. It opened in her hand to a page that must have been well-used quite recently—the page that listed the hotels in Liverpool! Several had been marked with a dot of biro. Her hand shaking, she slid it back into its place, and pulled out a paperback novel instead. Mike hadn't even glanced up.

Liverpool—yes, it made sense. It was a big town, with plenty of hotels—it would be hard to find them there, without any clues. It wasn't far away, either—now she thought about it, she remembered that Pete had mentioned that he occasionally went up there for a break. There were some of the best Chinese restaurants in the country, he had said. So—he had taken his lady-love to woo her with Szechuan chicken and water chestnuts!

But having worked that out, what good would it do her? She couldn't go looking for them—she hardly had any money, and, besides, Mike was bound to follow her. She didn't want that—she wanted to find them herself, talk to them, find out what was going on and persuade them to come back and face him and sort out this mess.

Maybe she could telephone instead. Pete had marked about half a dozen of the cheaper hotels—it shouldn't be too difficult to ring round them and find out which one he was staying at. She could slip out later, after pretending she had gone to bed—that way she could avoid any awkward questions from Mike.

Her plan made, the long evening was almost unbearable. The television commentary droned on, there were the small sounds—of the wood in the stove crackling, of the dogs snuffling around, of the wind bending the trees outside. But the telephone was silent. By nine o'clock Penny's nerves were as frayed as old rope. With studied nonchalance she yawned, and stood up.

'I think I'll turn in,' she said lightly. 'Goodnight.'

Mike only glanced up briefly from the screen, and murmured a terse, 'Goodnight.'

Safely in her bedroom, she carefully jammed the door shut with the chair as she had before, and then pulled the handbook out from beneath her pillow, where she had hidden it earlier, having sneaked it from the shelf and in to her room while Mike was in the bathroom. She had a phone-card in her purse, and plenty of coins—enough to be able to make quite a few calls. Enough to locate the runaways? She would just have to hope so.

The night air struck very cold as she eased open the narrow window. It wasn't snowing, but the chill wind was stirring flurries of snow that would quickly obliterate her footsteps, so even if Mike went out later with the dogs there would be nothing to give her away. She climbed out very carefully, and wedged the window shut behind her, and then, muffing her hands in the sleeves of her duffle-coat, she set off towards the village.

It was harder going than she had anticipated. She had thought the snow wasn't very deep—indeed, in most places it only just covered her ankles—but the wind had piled it into drifts across the path, and she found it tiring to flounder through it.

She slogged on doggedly, but as she left the shelter of the trees she was facing the teeth of the wind. Soon the very bones of her face were aching with cold, and fingers of ice were penetrating even into the warmth of her thick duffle-coat. Her boots, made for walking on city pavements, had begun to let in the wet, and her feet were growing numb.

The second time she stumbled and fell on her face into a drift, she began to realise that she had seriously misjudged the conditions. In London,

snow was a cause of only minor
inconvenience—the heat of the buildings made
heavy or prolonged falls rare. Although walking
could be slithery, there was rarely any danger of
coming to any serious harm—there was always
someone nearby to help, a warm place to shelter,
a bus to jump on.

But out here it was a very different matter. She
had been outside for barely ten minutes, but
already she was becoming exhausted. She had
read stories in the newspapers about people going
out in the snow and being found dead, but she
had always imagined that to be in the most
extreme conditions, not a fall of no more than
about eight inches. And it was only a mile or so
to the village.

Already she was disorientated—all around her
was just featureless white. And the cold was
seeping into her brain, making her long to lie
down and go to sleep . . . She would have to go
back—she could try to get to the village
tomorrow, maybe, if the snow thawed a little.

But the return journey seemed to be twice as
far as the way out. Her jeans were wet right up
to the thigh, and the hem of her duffle-coat was
dragging and heavy. Her woollen gloves were
soaking, and her fingers were like ice. Tears of
self-pity welled into her eyes. Why had she been
so stupid? She could have been tucked up in her
nice warm bed . . .

She stopped, just for a moment, and leaned
against the trunk of a tree. But as she closed her
eyes, her knees sagged, and she slid to the ground.
Wearily she tried to stand up again, but her body

just wouldn't obey her. It was so much easier just to lie here and sleep. Darkness rolled over her, and she let it sweep her consciousness away . . .

She mumbled a grumpy protest as someone disturbed her. It wasn't comfortable to be picked up—it made her head swim unpleasantly. Dimly she realised that it was Mike who was carrying her, and some part of her mind tried to remind her that he wasn't supposed to know that she was out here, but she really couldn't concentrate on that at the moment.

At least she didn't have to worry about getting back to the cottage any more—Mike would take care of everything, and she could just sleep . . . He was so strong, carrying her through the snow as if she weighed nothing at all. She let her head fall against his broad shoulder with a small grunt of contentment. All she wanted to do was sleep.

But he wouldn't let her sleep. He pushed open the cottage door, and set her on her feet in front of the wood-stove, and began to strip off her wet clothes. He seemed to be angry, but she couldn't quite work out why—her brain seemed to be filled with cotton wool. She couldn't even remember why she'd gone outside.

He stripped her down to her underwear. Vaguely she thought she ought to protest at such intimacy, but he didn't seem to be the least bit interested in admiring the slender curves of her body. His movements were brisk as he wrapped her up in the blanket he had slept in and sat her down in the armchair next to the fire.

She blinked in vague bewilderment, hugging the warm wool around her body, breathing the subtle muskiness that clung to it—a muskiness that reminded her acutely of being held in his arms. Slowly the chill was receding, and memory was coming back. There were going to be some awkward questions to answer.

He brought her a steaming mug of hot milk. She took it gratefully, cradling it in her hands, and lifted her eyes to his grim face. 'Th-thank you,' she murmured thickly.

'Warming up a bit now?' he enquired, little sympathy in his voice.

'Yes, thank you.'

'You could do with a warm bath, now the worst of the cold is wearing off. I'll run it for you.'

'Thank you.' She would have liked to apologise for causing him so much trouble, ask him how he had found her, but she didn't want to prompt him into asking her what she thought she had been playing at. It was safer to keep quiet for now, until her numb brain had had a chance to come up with some plausible excuse.

She heard the bath-water running, but when she stood up her head swam again, and she had to grip the back of the armchair to steady herself. And Mike was there again, his strong arm supporting her. 'Take it easy,' he reminded her. 'Would you like me to carry you again?'

'No—I can manage,' she assured him quickly.

He helped her as far as the bathroom door. 'I haven't run it too hot,' he told her. 'If you have any problems, call me. And don't stay in too long.'

She nodded humbly, and, after closing the door behind her, she unwrapped herself from the blanket, stripped off her underwear, and sank wearily into the bath. The warm water closed around her, easing the aching chill in her bones. With a sigh she closed her eyes, luxuriating in the sheer comfort of it. Her toes hurt a little as the circulation was restored, but it didn't trouble her. She had thought she would never be warm again.

It was hard to believe now that she had been in any real danger—she had gone barely half a mile, and the snow hadn't been deep at all. It had been the wind that had been the main problem really—the constant battle against it had exhausted her.

But the danger had been very real, a small voice reminded her. She must have been mad to go outside. If Mike hadn't come after her, she would be lying out there in the snow now, instead of in this nice warm bath. And that treacherous weariness that had come over her had been the first sign of hypothermia. Once she had fallen asleep, she would never have woken up. Mike had saved her life. Mike . . .

Her mind began to drift into the unchartered territory of dreams, weaving a fantasy around the real-life drama of what had happened. Instead of that cool indifference when he had stripped her clothes off, Mike had been aroused beyond all restraint by the sight of her near-naked body . . . She let her hands slide slowly down over her breasts . . . but in her dreams it was his hands that caressed her.

A sharp rap on the door startled her out of her reverie. 'Penny? Are you OK?'

'Oh . . . yes.' The bath-water swirled as she sat up quickly. She must have dozed off for a few moments—already it was starting to go cold. She jumped out, and reached for the big bath-towel. 'I won't be a minute.'

'Good. I've another cup of hot milk here for you.'

'Thank you.' She wrapped her wet hair up in a towel, and dried herself vigorously, and then drew the warm blanket around her shoulders again. When she opened the door, he was standing outside.

He surveyed her steadily. 'Yes, you look a little better,' he approved. 'Here, give me the towel and I'll dry your hair for you while you drink your milk.' She managed an uncertain smile, and he smiled back wryly. 'Later we'll talk about what you were doing out there.'

She lowered her eyes. So far she hadn't been able to come up with a single germ of an excuse for her foolhardy excursion. But he wasn't going to let her evade the issue—once he started questioning her, he was going to want answers.

She perched cross-legged on the edge of the bed, sipping her milk as he scrubbed her hair vigorously dry. She clutched the blanket tightly around her shoulders with one hand—it embarrassed her now, remembering that he had seen her in her underwear. She must have looked a pathetic sight, with her hair all bedraggled and her skin blue with cold. No wonder he had had no trouble at all in restraining his baser urges.

He finished drying her hair, and stepped back. 'There, that'll do. At least you won't catch pneumonia now.'

She shook the tumble of curls back around her shoulders. 'Thank you,' she said again, managing a tremulous smile. 'I've never been so cold in all my life.'

He laughed drily. 'You picked a fine place to lie down and go to sleep.'

'I know.'

She couldn't meet his eyes—the memory of the way he had scooped her up in his arms was too vivid in her brain. That immutable male strength that sometimes conveyed a subtle threat was at the same time a reassurance. He was a man to depend on . . . An odd little glow of heat had started, somewhere deep inside her. She found herself remembering the way he had kissed her . . .

Slowly she became aware of a strange tension shimmering in the air between them. She lifted her eyes, and saw that he was looking at her. The blanket had slipped slightly from one shoulder, revealing the soft curve of one small breast, delicately tipped with pink.

She heard him drag in a rugged breath, and then he looked away, the hard line of his mouth betraying the effort of will it cost him. Instinctively she reached out and touched his hand. He turned back to her, the flame in his eyes scorching into hers, warning her wordlessly. But her heart gave back only one answer.

With a small movement she shrugged the blanket back off her shoulders, a tremor of nervousness running through her as he let his gaze drift to linger over the naked swell of her breasts. She watched his face, silently pleading with him to accept her offer. The image of that other woman he loved rose to taunt her—but tonight, just this one night, she had her chance.

His eyes returned to hers, and a thrill scudded through her as she recognised the glowing intensity there. As she sat very still, his fingertips trailed slowly up her arm, and across her throat, and down into the soft valley between her breasts.

Her breath was warm on her lips as she gazed up into those mesmerising eyes. His hand curved beneath her breast, moulding its firm ripeness, his thumb brushing the taut, tender bud of her nipple. A shimmer of exquisite response ran through her, that she didn't try to hide.

And then at last, with a low groan of defeated will-power, his head bent over hers and he eased her back down on the bed. His mouth was hot on hers as he claimed her lips in a kiss that drove every other thought from her brain. His tongue swirled languorously over the delicate membranes within, plundering every secret depth, igniting fires that heated her blood.

The touch of his fingertips was a torment of pleasure as they fondled her warm, naked breasts, tracing a tantalising path around each tender peak until she was almost sobbing with anticipation, and then plucking gently at the hardened, sensitised buds, shafting an incandescent flame into her brain.

Too breathless for kisses, they broke apart, his lips moving over her eyelids, her temple, the delicate shell of her ear, and down the vulnerable column of her throat. Her spine curled in ecstasy, arching her body invitingly as he lifted her small breast in his hand, as if it were a ripe fruit, for his mouth to devour.

She opened her eyes, watching in a kind of burning fascination as his tongue lapped at the pink bud of her nipple, his teeth nibbling gently, driving her wild; and then he drew it deep into his mouth, suckling hungrily, pulsing a burning heat through her veins.

She reached for him urgently, brazen in her eagerness to touch him, to feel his rough male flesh against hers, and her fingers fumbled as she sought the buttons of his shirt. He laughed, low in his throat, teasing her for her wantonness, but she didn't care.

She managed at last, with a little help from him, and with a small sob buried her face against his hard chest, thrilling to the sound of his powerful heartbeat, which was pounding fast and hard. His weathered skin was a dark contrast to the soft translucence of her own in the subdued glow of the bedside lamp, his muscles strong and smooth beneath her hands.

The sheer male beauty of his body enthralled her, desire taught her things she'd never dreamed of. She pressed her lips against a throbbing pulse in the hollow of his wide shoulder, twined her fingers into the crisp curls that were scattered over his wide chest, traced the long cleft of his spine with one playful nail-tip.

He growled in fierce male response, crushing her deliciously beneath his weight. The blanket had fallen away, leaving her completely naked in his arms, and the rough denim of his jeans rasped against her skin, still warm and soft from her bath.

His hands slid down over her body in a gesture of demanding possessiveness, claiming every inch; the peach-smooth curve of her stomach, the dark downy mound that hid her most intimate secrets. The pleasure was almost too much to bear, spreading through her in a sweet, languid tide, and she parted her thighs in willing acquiescence as he sought the ultimate caresses.

She was melting in a warm tide of sensuality, moaning softly as his clever fingers did magical things to her. Dark fires were swirling around her, and she clung to him as if she were falling; he was the only reality in a world that had turned into dreams.

He shifted his weight to lie above her, showering her face with kisses. 'I want you, Penny,' he murmured, his voice husky and impeded. 'I've wanted you from the first moment I saw you.'

'Yes,' she whispered in urgent agreement, her heart filled with pure happiness as she surrendered to that primeval male demand.

But suddenly there was a sharp pain, and she couldn't hold back the cry that broke from her lips. He drew away from her with a fierce oath, and her eyes flew open in horror. He was glowering down at her, his face frozen into a mask of pure rage.

She reached for him in panic. 'Mike, please—don't stop,' she begged brokenly. 'I'm sorry, I didn't mean to scream—it's just that it's the first time for me, and I——'

'I'm fully aware of that,' he grated, rolling off the bed and fastening his jeans, buckling the heavy leather belt with aggressive impatience. He pulled open her holdall, which was on the floor, and dragged out a sweater and a spare pair of jeans, and tossed them at her in a gesture of pure contempt. 'Get dressed!' he ordered harshly.

'Mike . . .' She scrambled off the bed, trying to clutch at his arm, but he shook her off roughly.

'Get dressed,' he repeated. 'I want you in that kitchen in five minutes, and I want some answers—the truth this time. Otherwise, so help me, I'll choke the life out of you.' He looked down at her, and she shrank from the bitter anger in his eyes. 'Because, whatever else you are, you are *not* Pete Carter's wife.'

He went out, slamming the door with a force that reverberated through Penny's skull like thunder. She sank on to the bed, too shaken to think, or even to cry. Her body ached with the hollowness of unfulfilled desire, and she hugged the pillow fiercely as if to seek the solace that Mike had torn from her so abruptly.

At long last the pain subsided a little, and, drained of all feeling, her body began to respond to his last command. She dragged on her clothes, and pulled a brush through her tangled hair. And then, taking a deep, steadying breath, she pulled open the door to the living-room.

There were two mugs of coffee on the table, and Mike was sitting before one of them, his elbows on the table, his head sunk into his hands. Dumbly she sat down opposite him, and without looking at her he began the interrogation.

'OK, let's start with the easy ones. What's your name?'

'Penny Carter.'

'You're not married to Pete Carter.' It was a bald statement of fact.

'No.' She hesitated, and he waited. 'I'm his sister.'

There was a long silence before he spoke again, and when he did it was reluctantly, as if he didn't want to know the answer. 'How old are you?'

'Twenty,' she whispered almost inaudibly.

'Oh, my God,' he groaned, his fingers clenching as if he wanted to crush his own skull.

'Mike, I'm sorry,' she managed to say, her voice strangled by the obstruction in her throat.

'Sorry?' He lifted his head then, and stared at her, his eyes bleak. 'Do you have the slightest idea what you've done?'

'You don't have to think . . . you don't have to feel responsible for me,' she choked out, her eyes brimming with tears. 'Just because I'm so much younger than you. I knew what I was doing—I'm not a child.'

'And I'm not a cradle-snatcher!' he snapped back. 'Dammit, Penny, you're little more than half my age!'

'But you wanted me,' she pleaded urgently, reaching out instinctively to touch his hand. 'You did want me.'

'Yes, I wanted you,' he conceded, his jaw clenched. 'I'm flesh and blood. You make an offer like the one you made to me in there, and no man on earth could refuse. Even though I knew there was something wrong. You were too . . .

innocent, too inexperienced. You seemed almost surprised at what was happening.' He rose abruptly to his feet, and strode around the room, coming to a stop by the inglenook and bracing his hands on it, staring down moodily into the flickering flames in the wood-stove.

'I could learn,' begged Penny, hardly aware of what she was saying.

'Not with me,' he returned with swift finality.

She stared at his broad back, her heart torn with despair. Not even conscious of what she was doing, she rose to her feet and crossed over to him, putting out one trembling hand to touch the unyielding cliff of his shoulder. 'I love you, Mike,' she told him with all the intensity of feeling that was etched into her heart.

'Love?' He gave a sardonic laugh. 'You're far too young to know what you're talking about.'

'I'm not,' she protested, hurt. 'I mean it, Mike. Please believe me. Even though I had to lie to you about everything else, I'm telling the truth about that.'

He turned abruptly, and caught her wrist in a vicelike grip. 'Why did you lie, Penny?' he demanded roughly. 'Why did you pretend you were married to him?'

She closed her eyes for a moment against the anger that she saw in his, but then bravely opened them again and met his penetrating gaze squarely. 'He asked me to,' she said simply.

'And did you know why?' he persisted.

'Not at first.'

His grip on her wrist tightened so viciously, she thought he would snap the fragile bones, but then he almost threw her away from him and went back to the table and sat down, leaving her standing forlornly by the fireplace, rubbing her bruised wrist.

'So when did you find out?' he snarled.

'Only . . . only yesterday,' she stammered. 'When you told me . . . you said Pete had run off with another woman. Then it all made sense—I understood why he had left in such a hurry, why you were so angry.'

'Where were you going tonight?'

Guiltily she evaded his searching gaze. 'To ring him. You see . . . I'd cut the telephone wire.' Her confession was spoken in a small voice. 'He would have rung again tonight, and I knew that as soon as he found out you were still here he'd have come straight back, and . . . she'd have come with him. He's my brother, Mike,' she pleaded. 'No matter what was happening between us, my first loyalty had to be to him.'

The eyes he turned on her were as hard as rock. 'Go on,' he ordered tersely.

She hesitated, trying to find the words to explain 'It was to give him time, so that maybe . . . she'd choose to stay with him. But today . . . I've done nothing but think about it, and I realised that it was no good—that it was best to get it all sorted out as soon as possible.'

'So you do know where they are?' he grated.

She shook her head miserably. 'No. At least . . . I think they're in Liverpool—I found a motoring book with some hotels ticked off. I was going to ask him to come back, Mike, even if that meant . . . that she'd go back to you.' She blinked back the tears that were stinging the backs of her eyes. 'I know . . . you must love her very much.'

He lowered his head into his hands again in a gesture of total despair. Penny stood watching him, all her tenderness and compassion reaching out for him, but knowing he wouldn't welcome it. He didn't want her, and she wouldn't intrude on his pain by letting him hear her cry.

'Love her?' he said at last, his voice rough-edged. 'Yes, I love her—more than anything else in this world. But I don't think I ever thought to tell her. I bought her things . . . oh, lots of expensive presents, everything she wanted. But I was never there when she needed me—I was always too damned busy.'

He clenched his fist on the table. 'That's where your damned brother stepped in. He gave her attention where I'd neglected her—flattered her, sweet-talked her until he'd turned her head.' He laughed harshly. 'But she's hardly a woman—she's barely seventeen years old.' He looked up as Penny gasped in shock. 'She's my daughter.'

CHAPTER FIVE

THE floor came up and hit Penny a painful blow on the shoulder. When she opened her eyes, Mike was beside her, scooping her up in his arms. 'I think you've had enough for one night,' he said gruffly. He carried her to her room, and laid her on the bed. 'You'd better get some sleep—I want an early start in the morning.'

'We're going to find them?'

'Naturally. The snow's beginning to thaw already.' He stood looking down at her for a moment, and then put out his hand to brush away a tear that sparkled at the corner of her eye. She caught his hand, holding it against her cheek, pressing her lips against the strong pulse in his wrist. For an instant she thought he would return her caress, but then he pulled his hand away, and without a word he was gone.

She was too exhausted to think about the tangled implications of what she had learned. She took off her clothes and changed into her cotton nightdress, and climbed between the cool sheets. Sleep came quickly, but it was a restless, troubled sleep, stalked by nightmares.

She woke to find Mike shaking her gently awake. For a moment she was still in her dream-land, and reached for him with a smile of delight. But his grim expression brought her swiftly back to reality. 'What time is it?' she asked.

'Seven o'clock. Come on, get dressed—your breakfast will be ready in a minute.' His voice was brusque, and small lines of tension were etched around his eyes. Penny wondered if he had slept at all.

She sat up. 'Look, I . . . You don't really need me with you,' she suggested tentatively. 'Wouldn't it be better if I stayed here? There are the dogs, and the caravans to keep an eye on——'

'The dogs can come with us,' he said tersely. 'And the caravans can take care of themselves for a few days—I'm not leaving you here so you can ring up and warn him I'm coming, give him a chance to get away.'

'Oh . . .' She hung her head. She couldn't blame him for believing she would do that, even now that she knew the truth. 'All right,' she conceded reluctantly, 'I won't be long.'

As soon as he had closed the door she scrambled out of bed and had a quick wash, and then dressed in her jeans and the pink jumper she had worn on that first day—the day that Mike Wolfe had walked into her life. Could it really be only three days ago? It felt like a lifetime.

As she brushed her tumbled curls, she stared at her reflection in the mirror. It was still the same face—the same finely carved features, the same clear, creamy skin. But somehow there was a subtle difference now in those sapphire eyes, a trace of wistfulness in their misty depths.

Strangely, it had been easier when she had believed that her problem was a rival, some girlfriend, however formidable the competition.

Because he *had* been attracted to her, so she could always nurture even the tiniest hope that she stood a chance.

But now he believed that she was involved in some sort of plot concerning his daughter—and, even though she hadn't known what was happening, it was a charge she couldn't deny. And he would never forgive her.

What was Pete playing at? Why on earth had he run away with the girl? She had thought she knew him, but this seemed so out of character. He just wasn't the sort to take advantage of a young girl's innocence. Wearily she shook her head. If they managed to find them in Liverpool, she would have some answers.

She put the hair brush down, and went into the kitchen. Mike was already eating his breakfast. She sat down opposite him, and tried to smile. 'It looks as if most of the snow's gone now,' she remarked brightly. 'It didn't last long, did it?'

He looked at her, those hard hazel eyes telling her he wasn't interested in polite conversation.

'I'm sorry,' she murmured. 'I suppose you must be very worried about your daughter.'

'Did you know?' she asked.

'That it was your daughter? No, of course not,' she protested, stung.

He shrugged. 'It doesn't matter if you did nor not,' he said coldly.

'Mike, please! I didn't know,' she begged. 'I wouldn't have helped Pete lie to you if I'd known that.'

'Wouldn't you?' The caustic disdain in his eyes

was too much for her to meet, and she bowed her head. 'All right, I believe you,' he said at last. 'I doubt if you could have faked your reaction last night.' She looked up at him again, but his eyes were cold. 'Anyway, it's too late now,' he grated. 'It was probably too late before I even went to Africa.'

'What do you mean? Too late for what?'

'Don't be naïve!' he lashed at her.

Hot colour flooded her cheeks, but she leapt instantly to Pete's defence. 'How can you be so sure?' she protested angrily. 'Why should you assume that my brother has fewer scruples than you have?'

'He's a devious bastard,' he declared with conviction. His eyes slid over her in insolent appraisal. 'It was pretty clever of him to leave you behind as bait,' he sneered. 'After all, I could hardly object to him seducing my daughter when I'd seduced his little sister, could I?'

His words hurt every bit as much as he had intended them to. 'I can tell you don't know him very well,' she retorted bitterly.

'Our single encounter was mercifully brief.'

'Well, then!'

'You don't need to look into a sewer to know that it stinks.'

The sheer venom in his voice silenced her. There was no point in arguing with him. Pete had said that he was as obstinate as they come, and he had been right. He had convinced himself that, at seventeen, his daughter was too young to have a boyfriend, and nothing she could say was going to change his mind. He probably still thought of her as a little girl.

She finished her breakfast without another word, and then went to pack her things. She didn't want to go with him—it hurt too much, being close to him when everything was so wrong between them. But he had decided that she was going, and he was perfectly capable of enforcing his wishes.

The dogs were willing enough to pile into the cab of the truck. Penny scrambled up after them, before he could lift her—she'd had plenty of experience climbing in and out of trucks when hitch-hiking with Lizzie. This one was a luxurious one, she recognised at once—comfortably upholstered seats, air-conditioning, and a bunk in the back for the driver to sleep in on a long haul.

'Won't your firm wonder where you've been?' she enquired as he started the engine and swung the wheel to turn the long chassis on to the lane.

'They know where I've been.'

'Oh.' She pulled a wry face—clearly he wasn't going to make conversation easy. But it was going to take a couple of hours to drive to Liverpool, and she didn't fancy spending the whole journey in this bitter silence. 'Which part of Africa did you go to?' she persisted doggedly.

He sighed, but conceded an answer to her question. 'Mainly the famine region—Sudan, Chad, Burkina Faso.'

'What were you delivering?'

'Vaccines.'

She encouraged him to go on with a look of interested enquiry.

'It's a refrigerated truck,' he explained. 'It's the only way for the relief agencies to get the stuff out to some of the more remote places, where there's nowhere for a plane to land. And these babies are a bit expensive,' he added, patting the dashboard. 'It wouldn't be economical for them to keep one out there themselves, and maintenance would be a constant problem.'

'Oh, I see.' She regarded him covertly from beneath her lashes. He had spoken quite dismissively, as if it had been no more than a routine doddle down the motorway, but she had seen television reports about conditions out there. 'Do you go to Africa often?' she asked him.

'Not these days.' They had reached the village, and he had to focus all his attention on negotiating a narrow gap between parked cars. 'Your brother really picked his moment,' he went on bitterly. 'I got back to Dover, and rang the office to let them know I was on my way home, to be met with the pleasing intelligence that my daughter had eloped.

'Eloped?' Penny sat back in her seat, stunned. Had Pete intended to get married, without even telling her? And yet he certainly wasn't the type to lead a young girl into believing that that was what he intended unless he was really serious.

'You seem to have been as much in the dark about it as I was,' he commented in a dry tone.

'I was, but . . . Well, there you are—I told you Pete had scruples, too,' she reminded him triumphantly. 'I know she's a bit young, but if they want to get married——'

'Over my dead body,' he vowed savagely.

She blinked at him in astonishment. Certainly he had every right to be angry about it, but maybe if he hadn't been so unreasonable Pete wouldn't have been driven to such extremes. She felt a wave of pity for the couple—and for Mike. There was no doubt that he cared about his daughter very much, but his way of showing it had probably made him seem like some sort of tyrant.

'You know, I should imagine she must be a very grown-up seventeen,' she remarked carefully. 'My brother's no more a cradle-snatcher than you are.'

He snorted in angry derision. 'Oh, she's very grown-up in some ways,' he conceded wryly. 'She takes after her mother.'

'Your . . . your wife?'

'Ex-wife,' he corrected harshly. He was silent for a while, and then added with sad resignation, 'I'd hoped she wouldn't make the same sort of mess of her life as Gina did.'

Penny watched him, painfully compelled to know more. 'Gina?' she repeated, watching his reactions carefully. 'Was she Italian?'

'Half Italian.'

'Was she very beautiful?' she asked tentatively.

He laughed—a hard, unpleasant laugh. 'Oh, she was gorgeous! Huge dark eyes, a face like an angel, a fabulous body—every man's dream!'

'How did you meet her?' she persisted, an irrational twinge of jealousy stabbing at her heart.

He slanted her a sardonic glance. 'Are you going to keep on prying till you get the whole story?' he queried stingingly. 'It isn't a pretty, romantic tale, you know.'

Her dark lashes cast shadows over her pink cheeks. 'No . . . I . . .'

'She was sixteen when I met her,' he grated, the Geordie brogue in his voice returning strongly as he reminisced. 'Hell, I was only just seventeen myself. I was working for a big transport company in Jarrow—apprentice mechanic. I didn't have anywhere to live—my Mum had remarried and gone south, but I wouldn't go with them. Instead of getting a room, I used to sleep at the garage, in the back of one of the trucks.

'Gina's family lived just down the road, and she used to hang around the place a lot, flirting with the truckers. But she seemed to like me the best, and she took to slipping down late, when there was no one else around. She certainly kept me warm at night!' he added in a voice that left nothing to the imagination.

'One night her brothers came looking for her, and found us together, and there was hell to pay. But by then Clare was on the way anyway, so I was willing enough to marry her. I thought it was the right thing to do—so much for honourable intentions!'

He laughed with bitter self-mockery. 'Oh, it had its compensations at first,' he went on. 'All the cold and damp in Newcastle didn't do much to cool her blood! And then there was Clare.' His voice softened as he spoke of his daughter.

'What happened?' prompted Penny in a cautious whisper.

'You really want all the cheap and sordid details? All right—maybe it'll put a stop to your

silly infatuation.' Penny winced. 'We lived with
her parents to start off with. One room in a
crowded slum—it was sheer hell. Her parents
hated me for what I'd done to their precious
daughter, bringing shame on the family.

'In the end I couldn't take any more of it. I got
us a flat of our own, and made Gina come with
me. It was right on the other side of town. I
thought if I could get her away from her family,
we might stand a chance. But it didn't work out
like that.'

He fell silent for a minute, and then went on
heavily, 'With a home, and a wife and kid to
support, I needed money. Apprentices don't earn
a lot, and I was too young to drive a truck—you
have to be twenty-one to get a heavy goods
licence. But there are always people who want to
employ a good fast driver who won't ask too
many questions. I was lucky—first offence, I only
got eighteen months.'

Penny caught her breath, and he flickered a
sardonic glance towards her. 'You wanted to
know,' he reminded her.

'I . . . I'm sorry . . .'

He laughed harshly. 'Oh, it was my own
fault—I knew what I was doing.'

'Wh . . . what happened to your wife?' she asked.

His jaw set in a hard line. 'When I came out,
she'd left the flat. I couldn't find her at first—her
folks wouldn't tell me where she was. Then I
heard her name being bandied about in a local
café one night—it seemed that every Tom, Dick
and Harry in town knew her. Someone told me
where she was living, and I went straight round

there.

'There was no one in, but I could hear Clare
screaming, so I broke a window round the back.
It was the dirtiest hole you ever saw. Clare was
in her cot, with a filthy nappy on, breaking her
little heart. I cleaned her up as best I could, and
found some dregs of baby-food to give her. Then
I sat down and waited.

'Gina got back at about three in the morning,
with some bloke. She was so drunk, she could
hardly stand. There didn't seem much point
trying to have a rational discussion, so I just
knocked the guy across the street, picked up Clare
and walked out. I haven't seen Gina since.'

A long silence stretched between them. Penny
shifted uncomfortably in her seat, lost for words.

At last he said roughly, 'Well, aren't you going
to say anything?'

'What is there to say?' she responded flatly.

'You're not going to tell me that I should have
waited until the morning, given Gina a chance
to sober up? That I shouldn't have deprived her
of her daughter? That if I hadn't been stupid
enough to get myself slammed-up in the first
place, she'd never have done what she did?'

'How could I say that? You did what seemed
the only thing you could do at the time,' she
responded in a small voice. 'But . . . thank you
for telling me. I understand a little better now
why you think the way you do. It doesn't help,
but I understand.' The truck ground to a halt at
a road junction, and Mike turned to look at her.
She turned her head away to stare fixedly out of
the window, unable to meet those deep hazel

eyes. 'There are so many things against us,' she whispered sadly.

She felt the warmth of his hand over hers. 'There can't be any "us", Penny,' he murmured. 'You're just a kid. You don't understand what I'm trying to tell you.'

'No, I don't understand,' she whispered brokenly. 'I only know that I love you.'

'No, you don't.' He shook his head. 'I'm very flattered, but it's not love you feel. It's just a passing infatuation. When all this is over, you'll forget all about me in no time, and find someone of your own age. Then you'll be glad I didn't take you too seriously.'

Her mouth set into an obstinate line. He felt sorry for her, and she almost hated him for that. She drew her hand from his, tucked it under her arm, and continued to stare fixedly out of the window. After a moment he put the truck in gear, and turned it on to the main road.

The harsh beauty of the wintry landscape perfectly suited her mood. It was a hard land, the ancient granite crumpled into rugged mountains millions of years ago, the valleys carved by icy glaciers. There was still snow on the high ground, and the sky was a bleak grey. There were few signs of population—just the occasional stone cottage or farmhouse, a few scattered villages where roads and rivers crossed.

The trees that lined the twisting road were bare and stark against the sky. Come the warmth of spring, a million tender green leaves and bright flowers would clothe this gaunt, skeletal landscape, transforming it with youth and beauty. But she felt as though in her heart it would always be winter—she couldn't imagine that she could ever again be the blithely innocent girl who had left London just a few days ago.

It was some time before she noticed that the road-signs were not indicating the towns she had expected. 'Where are we going?' she asked, sitting up.

'To drop the truck off at the depot, and pick up my car,' he told her. 'We can hardly go searching round Liverpool in this. And, besides, it's not very practical to take the dogs—I'll get someone to look after them.'

'Oh. But I thought your depot was in Newcastle.'

'No, Walsall. It's a good spot—right by the motorway, central.'

'I see.'

They had reached Shrewsbury, with its endless series of roundabouts, and Penny watched in fascination as he negotiated the unwieldy vehicle around the obstacle course, shifting gears and swinging the large steering-wheel with deceptive ease, sparing a reassuring grin for the nervous pedestrians who gazed up in awe at the grunting, sighing monster.

At last they were back on a more or less straight road, that became a motorway a few miles further on. Penny settled back into the comfortable seat. The steady note of the engine, the soft cushioning of the suspension, the warmth in the heated cab all combined to produce a half-sleeping state, as she turned over and over in her mind everything he had told her.

She wasn't at all shocked by his revelations about his past—she felt only a deep sorrow that he had been driven to do what he had done. Instinctively she knew that he was as honest as he was caring, and she was sure that he had carried a weight of regret ever since. She shuddered at the thought of him confined in prison for all those months—he who was so free and proud. And when he had come out, there had been no soft, loving woman for him to go home to. If only . . . but it was too late to make it up to him now—many years too late.

She must have dozed off to sleep. She woke as the note of the engine changed, and the truck began to slow with a complaining hiss of air-brakes. They were leaving the motorway. Mike pulled the truck on to a roundabout, and down to a set of traffic-lights, and then on to a dual-carriageway. A few hundred yards further on they turned again, on to a concrete road that ran through an industrial estate, and came to a high chain-wire fence.

Beyond it, Penny could see the yard. It was a vast space, with room for dozens of vehicles. A few trucks and lorries and flat-backs were parked there, all in the same bright red livery as the one they were riding in. There was a workshop to one side, where several men were working on engines, and above it an office.

A uniformed security guard leaned out of the window of a small prefabricated hut beside the gates, saluting them with a cheerful wave as Mike swung the truck in a wide arc to pull through the gates. Penny was staring, her heart thudding in shock.

There was a huge wooden notice on the gates, painted red and black, and every truck bore the same logo on its side. Why hadn't she noticed it on this one? She hadn't even looked—it had never occurred to her. The name of the company was Wolfe International Transport.

Mike was watching her, his gaze coolly quizzical. 'Wh . . . why didn't you tell me?' she asked unsteadily.

'I thought you knew.'

She shook her head. 'Pete never said—not a word.'

'Well, now you can see why he was so keen to marry my daughter,' he sneered with biting sarcasm. He jumped down from the truck, and as he walked around the front of it she opened her door and scrambled down before he could offer any assistance. At once the dogs became excited, panting and scrabbling to get down. 'Stay,' he ordered them calmly, and closed the truck door on them.

Yes, and I bet you order everyone around like that, and expect such instant obedience, Penny thought angrily.

As if to prove her wrong, one of the mechanics strolled over to them, his greeting as casually informal as if they had been workmates, not employee and boss. 'Hi, Mike—have a good trip?' he asked.

'Not bad, Den.'

'Truck stand up OK?'

'Aye—the distributor packed up in El Djezair, but I managed to cannibalise something to get me home.'

'I'll fix it.'

Mike tossed him the keys. 'Do us a favour,' he added genially. 'There's a mobile zoo in the back—find them a safe place for a couple of days, would you?'

The mechanic climbed on to the step of the truck and peered into the cab. 'What have you been doing?' he asked, laughing. 'Collecting waifs and strays?'

'Something like that. Come on, Penny.'

The mechanic cast her a glance of cursory interest, and her mouth set in a thin line. Yes, I bet I look just like some out-at-elbows stray he's collected too, she reflected angrily—some hitch-hiker he's picked up, who's paid her fare on the bunk in the back of the cab. She shouldered her bag, and followed Mike up the stairs and into the offices.

They passed through a pair of glass doors into a smartly carpeted reception area, where a pretty blonde with inch-long pink fingernails welcomed him pertly. 'Hell, Mike. Nice to see you back—we all missed you.'

He laughed. 'Angling for a rise, Sharon?' he teased.

'No ... Well, if there's one going ...? She batted a pair of sooty eyelashes at him. Penny felt her jaw clench.

'Not this month,' he retorted, pushing through another pair of glass doors into a large open-plan office with sunny yellow walls and masses of thriving pot-plants.

Penny tilted her chin in the air, ignoring the

receptionist's insolent curiosity, and followed him. A flurry of warm greetings welcomed him as he walked past the desks, and he returned them all, asking after sick children and errant boyfriends as he went. Plainly he was a very popular boss—yet the room hummed with efficiency, green computer-screens flashing and telephones buzzing, everyone getting on with their jobs even as they spared a moment to say hello.

He pushed open another door, and a willowy blonde secretary turned from a filing cabinet, a smile of rather special intimacy curving her scarlet lips. 'Mike—oh, thank goodness you're safely back,' she said, coming over to him. 'Was it all right?'

'Why, aye then,' he assured her, giving her shoulders a squeeze. 'Were you worrying about me then, Frankie?'

'Of course I was. It could have been dangerous—you didn't have to go yourself.'

'Oh, aye? You reckon I should have sent one of the lads out, and sat here at my desk, like?'

She shook her head, laughing. 'Oh, I know you couldn't have done that,' she conceded. 'But now there's this awful business with Clare . . .' Her voice had dropped to a low tone, and she leaned close to him, putting her hand on his arm as she spoke. Penny stood by, feeling awkward and foolish—how very predictable, that he would be having an affair with his elegant secretary.

'Aye, well, I think I could be on to something. Get me some coffee, Frankie, and get me a list of all the hotels and boarding-houses in

Liverpool—any place to stay. I'll be going up there, maybe for a couple of nights—see to the reservations, would you?'

'Of course.' For the first time the woman seemed to notice Penny, and her cool grey eyes swept over her disparagingly.

Mike didn't bother to introduce her. 'Have the import licences come through for that load for the Philippines yet?' he asked.

'They're on your desk. Also the time schedules for the Watson contract, and the tenders for Dean Chemicals.'

'Good. Anything else?'

'Doug wants to talk to you about the lease on the new warehouse, and the union wants to discuss the factory inspector's report.'

'Right—tell Doug to come through in fifteen minutes, and make an appointment with the shop stewards' committee for Monday morning.'

'Yes, Mike.' She was at once the efficient secretary again, but behind his back she favoured Penny with another icy appraisal. 'Er . . . will it be *two* cups of coffee?' she enquired with a haughty lift of one finely drawn eyebrow.

'Yes, please. Deal with that first, and then get on to the other things. Come on, Penny.'

Penny returned the woman's frosty glare in kind, and followed him into his own office. It was a light, spacious room; windows on two sides overlooked the wide sweep of the busy motorway, but they were double-glazed to deaden the noise and tinted to soften the glare of the sun. The carpet was a restful shade of steel-blue, and the furniture black ash, with several deep leather armchairs gathered in a conversation pit around a low table at the opposite end of the room from the massive desk.

She stood gazing around, trying to come to terms with all the surprises of the past five minutes. The rugged truck-driver she had known for the past three days didn't exist; the real Mike Wolfe was a successful businessman—a *very* successful one, by the look of it.

It was just about the last straw. Wearily she sank into one of the armchairs, and closed her eyes. Even if she could have convinced him that the age-gap wasn't as bad as he thought, even if the problems with Pete could have been resolved—even if his secretary decided to emigrate—the barrier between them would still be insurmountable.

A rich man might indulge in a casual fling with a pretty, penniless girl like her from time to time, but he wouldn't take it seriously. Maybe she should just settle for what she could get—a brief affair, nothing more. She slanted him a covert look from beneath her lashes.

Could she do that? Just go to bed with him, and then let him walk away from her? Maybe it would be worth all the pain, even for just one night of pure happiness. Or would it be like trying to put out a fire by dousing it with a can of petrol?

This lovely Victorian pewter-finish miniature is perfect for displaying a treasured photograph— and it's yours absolutely free—when you accept our no-risk offer.

PLAY "LUCKY 7"

Just scratch off the silver box with a coin.
Then check below to see which gifts you get.

YES! I have scratched off the silver box. Please send me all the gifts for which I qualify. I understand I am under no obligation to purchase any books, as explained on the opposite page.

106 CIH AC7G

NAME

ADDRESS   APT

CITY   STATE   ZIP

7	7	7	WORTH FOUR FREE BOOKS, FREE VICTORIAN PICTURE FRAME AND MYSTERY BONUS
🍒	🍒	🍒	WORTH FOUR FREE BOOKS AND MYSTERY BONUS
●	●	●	WORTH FOUR FREE BOOKS
🔔	🔔	🍒	WORTH TWO FREE BOOKS

Offer limited to one per household and not valid to current Harlequin Presents® subscribers. All orders subject to approval.
Terms and prices subject to change without notice.
© 1990 HARLEQUIN ENTERPRISES LIMITED

PRINTED IN U.S.A.

DETACH AND MAIL CARD TODAY

DETACH AND MAIL CARD TODAY

BUSINESS REPLY MAIL

FIRST CLASS MAIL   PERMIT NO. 717   BUFFALO, NY

POSTAGE WILL BE PAID BY ADDRESSEE

HARLEQUIN READER SERVICE
3010 WALDEN AVE
PO BOX 1867
BUFFALO NY 14240-9952

NO POSTAGE
NECESSARY
IF MAILED
IN THE
UNITED STATES

CHAPTER SIX

'I'M GOING to take a shower,' Mike announced bluntly, cutting across her thoughts. 'I won't be long.'

He vanished through a barely noticeable door behind his desk. A few moments later the other door opened, and the secretary came in, carrying a tray on which were a silver coffee-pot, two mugs of expensive plain white china, a silver sugar-bowl and a plate of chocolate biscuits.

'Sugar?' she enquired in a tone of distilled condescension.

Penny returned her cold look levelly. 'No, thank you,' she responded, hostility adding an edge to her voice.

Those scarlet lips curved into a thin smile. 'Where did Mick pick you up?' she enquired in spurious friendliness.

'In Wales,' Penny told her—if Mike hadn't chosen to explain her presence, she certainly wasn't going to do so.

'Oh, really? And where are you heading?'

'Liverpool—for now.' Some evil demon prompted her to put on a casual, slouching air, as if she really was the sort of girl who regularly let herself be picked up by truck-drivers and was quite ready to pay her fare in the oldest currency of all.

'Really?' The scarlet smile had become rather brittle.

Penny sat forward, grabbing for the chocolate biscuits as if she had never been taught manners. 'Great—I'm starving,' she announced, letting a broad strain of common-sounding cockney slip into her accent. The secretary drew back as if there was an unpleasant smell under her nose, and Penny suppressed a smile of satisfaction—at least she had succeeded in ruffling those sleek feathers a little.

Was she having an affair with Mike? She was very much the type Penny had envisaged—late twenties, very cool and efficient, but with enough subtle hints to remind any red-blooded male that she was all woman. She was wearing several good rings, but none of them on her wedding finger. Divorced, like himself, perhaps—that would suit him perfectly.

Both women glanced up sharply as Mike emerged from the dressing-room, his hair still slightly damp from his shower. He had changed into a well-cut grey business-suit that elegantly moulded his powerful shoulders, and was deftly knotting a pink silk tie over a pale grey cotton shirt. He looked every inch the wealthy business tycoon—and yet . . . there was still that hint of raw maleness about him, something slightly untamed beneath that urbane exterior.

'Ah, coffee. Thanks, Frankie.' He moved over to sit at his desk, and picked up a sheaf of papers. 'Are these licences all in order?'

'Yes, Mike. I checked them myself.' She fetched his coffee, even stirring the sugar in for him, and took it over to him, leaning a little closer than was quite necessary to point something out to him.

'Whatever would I do without you?' he enquired lightly, taking a slim gold pen from his pocket to sign the sheets.

Over his head the woman flashed Penny a small smile of triumph. 'Doug's here,' she added to him.

'Fine—send him in.' He glanced over at Penny. 'I'll be a while here,' he said. 'You can have a freshen-up, if you like.'

'Thank you.'

She was glad to be able to retreat. The door behind the desk opened into a well-appointed dressing-room, carpeted in the same steel-blue as the office and lit by concealed fluorescent strips. Sliding mirrored panels revealed a neat bathroom with a shower, and a wardrobe stocked with several changes of clothing.

She flicked along the rail. There was no rubbish here—the suits were all Savile Row, the shirts hand-made by Turnbull and Asser. With a small sigh she closed the wardrobe. How much evidence did she need? She had known from the start that she was a fool to fall in love with him, but it didn't help—nothing helped.

If only, last night . . . That hollow ache returned, so acute that it was almost a physical pain. Just by closing her eyes she could relive every moment, as vividly as if he were there now, his kisses deep and demanding, his clever hands caressing her body . . .

She drew a deep breath, struggling to pull

herself together. The thoughts in her brain had heated her blood—what she needed was a nice, cooling shower. Quickly she stripped off her clothes, and stepped into the bathroom.

It was soothing to let the warm needles of water splash down over her skin. She found some shampoo and washed her hair, and then, wrapping herself up in a big towel, sarong-style, she padded back into the dressing-room. There was a hair-dryer in the bottom of the wardrobe—who used that? The secretary, perhaps, when he was taking her out to dinner after they'd been working late? There were some women's clothes in the wardrobe, too, the kind of thing the elegant blonde would wear.

She was sitting on the floor, scrunch-drying her tumbled curls, when there was a peremptory tap on the door and Mike pulled it open.

'Just walk in, why don't you? she snapped crossly, glaring up at him.

He hesitated on the threshold, but his secretary was across the room, trying to peer through the open door. He stepped inside, closing it firmly behind him. 'I'm sorry,' he grated tersely. 'I didn't realise you were taking a shower.' There was an unmistakable tension in the line of his jaw, and he was having considerable difficulty keeping his eyes from the soft curves of her breasts, wrapped by the towel.

Good! she thought fiercely. Let him feel uncomfortable too. 'What did you want?' she asked coldly.

'I'll be ready to go in a few minutes.'

'Well, why don't you just whistle at me?' she

suggested, her voice dripping sarcasm. 'Maybe I'll run to heel, like the dogs.'

A dangerous glint lit his hazel eyes. 'If you'd told me the truth three days ago, this wouldn't be necessary,' he pointed out.

'If you'd told me it was your daughter . . .' she countered defiantly.

'Was I supposed to tell you your husband had run away with another woman? How did I know how you'd react? You might have become suicidal!'

'What a typical male attitude! The helpless little woman, going to pieces just because a man had run out on her!'

'I'm glad to know you're tougher than that,' he returned, his tone underlining his meaning. 'Now, if you wouldn't mind getting dressed—please—we can get up to Liverpool and try and sort out this unholy mess.'

He withdrew, pulling the door shut behind him, but not before Penny had caught sight of his secretary's sour face. She might have heard raised voices, but her mouth thinned into a hard line when she saw Penny wearing nothing but a towel.

Penny felt a glow of grim satisfaction. At least the older woman wasn't completely sure of her position—Mike had made no commitment to her. One experience of commitment had probably been more than enough for him. What was it he had said about taking what was offered?

Maybe she should do that, too. Just once, just for the short time she had left with him. Whatever he had said, whatever his suspicions about her, she knew that he still wanted her—the look in his eyes told her that, more clearly than any words he could have spoken.

She stood and stared at her reflection in the long mirror. Could she make a decision like that—to surrender to a man whom she knew cared nothing about her? Last night she could at least claim the excuse that in the burning heat of the moment she hadn't been thinking at all. But now . . .

She shook her head, trying to shake the confusion from her brain. This wasn't the time for such a debate—Mike would be getting impatient to start for Liverpool. She got dressed quickly, pulling on her jeans and a clean jumper, and combed her hair into some semblance of order. And then, taking a deep breath, she pushed the door open.

Mike barely glanced at her. 'Ah, you're ready,' he said tersely. 'Right, Frankie, you know where to find me. I'll keep in touch.'

'Of course, Mike. I hope you find her safely.' She put up her hands to make a quite unnecessary adjustment to his tie—an oddly intimate, possessive gesture that set Penny's teeth on edge.

She held her head up as they walked back through the main office, ignoring the interested stares that followed her. Mike led her down the steps and round to the side of the workshop. The dogs were there, confined in a small side-office, and they began to bark excitedly as soon as they saw her.

She went over to make a fuss of them. 'Goodbye, now,' she murmured. 'Be good. I'll be back for you soon.'

'Everything OK?' Mike asked the mechanic.

'Of course. I rang the missus—she grumbled a bit, but she won't mind having them for a few days.'

'Good. Thanks, Den. Come on then, Penny, let's get going.'

There were several cars parked beside the workshop, but she knew at once which was his—it had his personality written all over it. A big, bullish Aston Martin with great thick tyres and sleek, muscular lines—one of the fastest cars on the road, but definitely not for the inexperienced driver.

He held the door for her, and she climbed in. The interior was beautiful, with piped leather seats that moulded her body in superb comfort, and a burr-walnut dashboard with businesslike round dials instead of the fancy digital things found on less classic boy-racer sports cars.

She could feel the power in the engine as soon as he turned the ignition—not a showy, deep-throated roar, but a muted rumble—and the car almost drifted away from a standstill, smoothing up through the gears as he swung out on to the main road, accelerating with elegant ease as he pulled on to the motorway, moving straight out into the fast lane, gathering speed to seventy, but still with more than half its performance in reserve.

'What a fabulous car!' she breathed.

He spared her a sardonic glance. 'It doesn't

generally appeal to women,' he remarked. 'They tend to go for my Rolls or the Porsche.'

'How many cars have you got?' she enquired drily.

'Six, the last time I counted.'

She let her upper lip curl into a slight sneer. 'What's the point of having six cars?' she retorted. 'You can't drive them all at once.'

'True—but we all have our little vices. Mine's collecting cars.'

'It's a shame you can't think of anything better to do with your money!' she snapped back.

'Like what? Letting your brother relieve me of some of it?'

She shot him a fulminating glare. 'Pete won't want a penny from you,' she spat.

'No? Why else does he want to marry my daughter?'

'Pete was right,' she sighed in exasperation. 'You're the most obstinate person I've ever met. I suppose it would never occur to you that he might be in love with her?'

'A kid half his age?' he sneered. 'Don't be ridiculous.'

She stared at him helplessly. What could she ever say to convince him? And it didn't take a pocket calculator to work out that the difference between the ages of seventeen and twenty-nine was rather less than that between twenty and thirty-five. He couldn't have spelled out more clearly that she hadn't a hope.

'Anyway, he can't marry her,' she pointed out coldly. 'Not if she's only seventeen, not without your consent.'

'I'm perfectly well aware of that—and so, I'm sure, is he. Presumably he thinks that I'd rather accept it as a *fait accompli* than create a scandal by having it annulled.'

Penny sat back in her seat, shaken. Surely Pete couldn't be planning such a devious scheme?

'I got a shock when I got to the cottage and found you there,' he told her, an edge of bitterness in his voice. 'That was very clever of him—you were sand in my eyes, in more ways than one. If you hadn't been there, I'd have taken steps immediately to have her made a ward of court.' He slanted her an angry glance, and she lowered her eyes guiltily. It was her lies that had diverted him from protecting his daughter.

'But your presence put me off the track,' he went on, his jaw clenched with anger. 'It didn't seem likely that he'd risk committing bigamy—that's an imprisonable offence, and it would have rendered the marriage null whatever I may have thought about it. So it looked as if he'd just taken her off for a dirty weekend—which is probably no more than they've been doing for weeks anyway. Oh, I know there's nothing unusual in that these days, but a man can't help hoping that his own daughter . . .'

Penny stared down at her hands, clenched in her lap. She was sure that he was wrong about that. But it must be any rich man's nightmare that his daughter would fall prey to a fortune-hunter. She couldn't really blame him for believing that Pete was one. 'Wh . . . what will you do now?' she asked hesitantly. 'I mean . . . if they've already . . .'

'I don't know.' He seemed almost defeated. 'If he had been married already, it would have been easy. I knew that nothing I could say would open Clare's eyes to him, but once she saw you—well, she'd have known he was just making a fool of her. I should have guessed there was something wrong—if a man had a wife like you, he wouldn't go running around after other women.'

The remark, so unthinkingly delivered, almost took Penny's breath away. She stared at him, wondering if he had even realised what he had said. But his attention was all on the road as the powerful car overtook everything in sight. His hands were clenched on the wheel, the knuckles white.

'Maybe I can't make her understand,' he grated. 'But when I find him, I'm going to take him limb from limb.' He spelled each word out slowly, like single drops of pure acid.

Penny shivered, knowing that he was perfectly capable of carrying out his threat. 'You're so wrong about Pete,' she said sadly. 'Just give him a chance—you'll see. He won't want anything from you—he'll support her himself.'

'How?'

'He's got a job.'

'Not after this, he hasn't. You think I'd keep him on?'

'*You?*' Oh, that was a cruel twist. 'You mean *you* own the caravan site?'

'That's how she met him—she went down there for a spell in the summer, with her grandmother—who doesn't seem to have kept much of an eye on her.' He lifted one eyebrow in mocking enquiry. 'Didn't he tell you that, either?' he taunted. 'He doesn't seem to have taken you very much into his confidence.'

'He wouldn't need to,' she countered, her jaw set as she gazed straight ahead. 'I'd always trust him—I know he'd never do a selfish or unkind thing in his life.'

'Such touching faith,' he drawled with a sneer.

'I hate you,' she whispered tensely.

He shrugged his wide shoulders in a gesture of pure indifference. 'That's progress—you seem to be recovering from your brief infatuation already.'

She turned away from him, tears stinging her eyes. How could she ever make him understand? He had convinced himself that his daughter was setting out on the same destructive path as her mother. Of course, he had every reason to be concerned, to feel that she was far too young to take on the responsibility of marriage. But if only he'd taken the trouble to get to know Pete before condemning him out of hand.

Penny had to acknowledge that she was biased, but she knew that Pete would take very good care of his child bride. On reflection, she felt it was just right for him, and for the unknown Clare. But Mike Wolfe wasn't the type to engage in quiet reflection—she could well imagine him hitting the roof as soon as he learned that his daughter even had a boyfriend, let alone that she was being seriously courted by a man of nearly thirty.

Poor kid—no wonder she'd ducked and run. And in the circumstances, all Pete's protective

instincts would urge him to make her his wife, so
that he could defend her from her bullying father.
What a mess! Still, it wasn't irreparable. If they
had married, even though it was illegal Mike
would probably have to be pragmatic about it.
And once he came to realise how good and
dependable Pete really was, he'd change his
attitude.

The big engine ate up the miles of motorway
with ease, the suspension giving a surprisingly
soft ride for such a brute of a car. Penny let
herself be carried to the fringes of sleep, aware
only of the man beside her. With her eyes closed,
she could feel the animal warmth radiating from
his body, stirring her senses on a level too deep
to control.

Her body reminded her of the feel of his
caressing hands, and she ached to feel that touch
again. And he wanted her. He might be having
an affair with his secretary, but he wanted her.
He might have scruples about taking advantage
of her youth and innocence, he might think she
was tarred with the same brush as her brother,
but that look in his eyes when he had seen her
wrapped in the towel had told her all she needed
to know.

Dreams swirled in her brain, dreams in which
all the barriers between them were set aside. He
would come to her, scoop her up in those strong
arms, and nothing would matter but the urgent
need that drove them both. He would kiss her,
undress her . . .

She jerked awake, suddenly hot, almost afraid
that he had been aware of the images she had

been conjuring in her mind. But he was looking straight ahead, his eyes seeing every changing pattern in the traffic, his hands controlling the leather steering-wheel with cool authority.

'Are we nearly there?' she asked.

'Aye.'

'Are we going through the Mersey Tunnel?'

'No.'

'Great conversationalist, aren't you?' she muttered crossly.

'In case you've forgotten, I've things on my mind.'

That silenced her. Those barriers would not be so easily set aside.

The motorway ended, and soon they were driving into town. The traffic was quite heavy, but Mike seemed to know exactly where he was going. Penny gazed around with interest, catching sight of the striking conical outline of the Catholic cathedral over the roofs of the university buildings, fascinated by the panorama of the city and its river spread before them.

'We'll just book in and leave our bags,' said Mike as he swung the car in front of Liverpool's most prestigious hotel. 'I want to start looking right away.'

Penny glanced wryly up at the elegant façade. 'I doubt if they'll let me in, dressed like this,' she mused, conscious of the scruffy appearance of her duffle-coat and jeans.

He laughed shortly. 'They won't take any notice—they have plenty of show-business and sports people staying here, who aren't always renowned for their smartness.'

'Have you stayed here before, then?'

'I sometimes have business up here,' he explained.

She climbed out of the car as he took his own well-travelled leather overnight bag and her canvas holdall out of the boot, and followed him up the steps and through the revolving door. As if to underline what he had predicted, the foyer was crowded with a noisy bunch of young men in yellow tracksuits, some of them slouching on their kitbags on the floor.

But the hotel was every bit as elegant as she had anticipated. As Mike booked in at the reception, she wandered over to peer through some glass doors, and found herself almost stepping back in time, into a vast lounge laid out with parlour palms and chintz and cane furniture beneath a high glass ceiling. She could almost see the rich Edwardian ladies in their bustles and feathers, sipping tea . . .

'Penny . . . come on, we don't have time for you to stand there day-dreaming.'

'Aren't we going to have lunch first?'

'Lunch?'

'Yes, lunch. It's gone one o'clock, and I'm starving.'

He raised his eyes in an expression of exasperation. 'Oh, all right,' he conceded grudgingly. 'I suppose we've got time to have a quick bite. Come on, then.'

'You're so gracious,' she muttered tartly as she followed him down to the restaurant.

'Oh, I'm so sorry.' He bowed in mocking gallantry as he held out a chair for her. 'Would you do me the honour of having lunch with me?' He was still irritated, but he seemed faintly amused by the way she was standing up to him.

She favoured him with a cool smile. 'Thank you,' she responded with dignity, picking up the pink linen napkin and spreading it on her lap.

They spent the entire afternoon combing the city without success. By evening Penny was tired and despondent, and Mike morose. 'It's beginning to look as if we've come on a wild-goose chase,' he growled as they drew a blank at yet another hotel.

'I told you, you're looking in all the wrong places,' she reminded him impatiently—he hadn't listened to a word of advice from her all afternoon. 'Pete wouldn't be able to afford to stay in a hotel for more than one or two nights—after that they'd probably have moved to a cheaper bed-and-breakfast place.'

'Oh? You think he'd be tactful enough to leave Clare's allowance alone until he's safely tied the knot?' he asked acidly.

She returned him an icy glare. 'If you're going to twist everything I say, I'm not going to bother to speak to you,' she warned angrily.

He heaved a weary sign. 'Oh, well, you could be right,' he conceded. 'But this town's riddled with cheap bed-and-breakfast places. 'It'll be like finding a needle in a haystack. Still, we'd better give it a try.' He pulled open the car door, but Penny finally rebelled, and stood stock-still in the middle of the pavement, her arms folded. 'Now what's wrong?' he demanded.

'I'm hungry.'

'Oh, for goodness' sake!'

'I have had *enough* of you,' she stormed. 'Ordering me around—who do you think you are? I'm not getting into this car again. I want something to eat, and I'm going to get it.' She turned on her heel, and stalked down the road towards a hot-dog stand—the smell of food, however greasy and unpalatable, was making her mouth water.

Mike caught up with her after a few yards, and took her arm. 'All right, I'm sorry,' he conceded tersely. 'I'm hungry too—maybe we ought to call it a day now. And didn't you mention that your brother's keen on Chinese food?'

Penny stared at him, and then burst out laughing. 'It's no wonder you've made your fortune,' she told him. 'I've never met anyone so single-minded.'

He laughed too. 'I know—I'm sorry. I've often been accused of it—especially by Clare. Maybe I'd better try and change,' he added wryly. 'I only set out to make enough to give her security and a bit of comfort, but instead it's kind of taken over. I didn't see what was happening—my daughter's grown up, and I didn't even notice. And now it's too late.'

The bleak sorrow in his voice wrung Penny's heart. 'Oh, no,' she protested, instinctively putting out a hand to touch his arm. 'I'm sure it's not. Once we find them, you'll see, you'll be able to sort it out with her.'

'I hope so.'

Suddenly she felt awkward with her hand on his arm. She drew it away quickly, and turned back towards the car. He held open the door for her, and she slid into the passenger seat, watching as he walked round the bonnet to climb in behind the wheel.

Anxiety was etched into every line of his face—it had increased as every hour had passed without finding his daughter. She found herself growing quite angry with Pete—what on earth did he think he was doing? He couldn't marry the girl until she was eighteen, so why didn't he just take her back home, and wait till then? It wasn't such a long time.

They drove back towards the centre of town, past the skeleton of a bombed-out church that had been cleaned up and had its clock repaired— a contradiction that made Penny smile. This city was full of contradictions—everywhere there were signs of a bold spirit holding back the encroachment of dereliction.

Mike parked the car at the kerb, and came round to open her door. They were in a wide, busy street, which was rather scruffy and undistinguished—except that at least half the shop-signs bore colourful Chinese characters. 'This used to be the heart of Chinatown,' Mike told her. 'There's not much of it left now, but it's still the best place to eat a proper Chinese meal.'

He led her round a corner, through a door, and up a narrow, precipitous flight of stairs. She looked around with some misgiving—the place had the air of a rather unprepossessing café. But as he pushed open a door painted with cheap blue gloss, they stepped into another world.

Three rooms, of irregular shape and differing heights, had been knocked into one, linked by arches. The soft lights from colourful paper lanterns cast diffuse shadows, lending an air of warmth and intimacy to the place. The tables were round, covered by plain red cloths, and each bore a candle in a pretty china bowl, which lit the faces of the diners with a flickering glow.

It was clearly a very popular place—one corner was occupied by a lively group of students from the university, but there was also a number of people who could well have afforded to dine somewhere much more expensive, and several whom Penny recognised from her television screen.

A white-coated waiter with pure oriental features and a rich scouse accent greeted them politely, and led them to a corner table. As he brought them the menu, Mike delayed him a moment, drawing out his wallet. 'Have you seen this girl?' he asked, showing him a photograph and a casual glimpse of the folding money inside. 'She might have been here in the past few days, with a young man.'

The waiter hesitated. 'What's up?' he asked. 'You the fuzz, or what?'

'No,' put in Penny, leaning forward, turning on him the full kilowatt power of her sapphire-blue eyes. 'She's his daughter, and the man's my brother. We need to get in touch with them. Please—have they been here?'

The waiter conceded a smile, not immune to her persuasion. 'They was in here on Tuesday night,' he admitted, discreetly accepting the tip

Mike tucked into his hand. 'I wouldn't forget a pretty girl like that.'

'Thank you.' Mike leaned back in his chair and regarded Penny with a sardonic smile. 'Well, it looks as if we haven't come on a wild-goose chase, after all,' he said,

CHAPTER SEVEN

'MAY I see the photograph?' she asked diffidently.

He handed it across the table to her, and she studied with interest. It was of a strikingly attractive girl—her Italian blood showed in her vivid colouring and the soft fullness of her lips, but her determined jaw she had inherited straight from her father. She looked older than seventeen—as he had said, she had matured early, like her mother.

She could understand Mike's anxiety. She was a girl who would attract the sort of attention no father would want for his seventeen-year-old daughter—and she looked as if she was strong-willed, and could be hard to control. Again she reflected that he was lucky that it was Pete she had fallen in love with, before some far less honourable Romeo swept her off her feet. But would Mike ever see it like that?

And now he knew that they were here in Liverpool, and he wouldn't rest till he had found them. She shivered—she would prefer not to be present when the two men finally came face to face. But she had a feeling that she wouldn't be able to avoid it.

She handed the photograph back to him. 'She's very pretty,' she remarked softly.

He glanced down at the picture, and there was

a warmth in his eyes. 'Yes, she is, isn't she?' he mused, putting it back in his wallet.

'What did you do after you left your wife?' she asked him. 'Where did you go with Clare?'

He didn't answer her at first—the waiter had returned to take their orders, and then the wine-waiter came. But when they were alone again he began without further prompting. 'I took her to my mum's—she'd moved down to the Midlands when she got married again. I hadn't been too keen on her doing that—see, my dad was a fireman, and he was killed when I was about ten. As far as I was concerned, he was a hero, and there was no way she should marry someone else.'

He smiled wryly. 'But I guess I got a bit more understanding as I grew older,' he went on. 'Actually, my stepfather's a great bloke. They took us in, and my mum looked after Clare while I was working—as soon as I could I got on the heavy-goods trucks. There was more money in it, especially on the long runs abroad.'

'What made you decide to set up in business for yourself?' she asked.

'I never really intended to. But the firm I was working for was going broke, and men were being put out of jobs for want of a bit of common sense in running the thing. I'd got a bit put by—I'd been saving all I could, planning to buy a little place for me and Clare when she got a bit older and started school.

'But it seemed like a better idea to put it into buying up the firm. My mum and my stepfather backed me—they even took out a second mortgage to lend me some cash, and the bank manager was a lot of help, too. I managed to keep on most of the old drivers, and as things got better I was able to take on a couple of my brothers as well, to help run things.

'It's a funny thing,' he mused, half to himself. 'I never set out to be a millionaire—all I ever wanted was to provide a cushion of security for Clare, so that I'd never be reduced to . . . what I was when she was a babe.' A shadow passed across his face.

'But one thing led to another—well, you get to hear a lot of inside information in this business. I tried buying a few shares when I had some spare cash, and I did pretty well out of that. Then there were one or two other small businesses that I knew had a lot of potential if they were properly run.'

'And before you knew where you were, you were a high-powered businessman with a vast empire under your control,' she teased.

He smiled, shaking his head. 'Not vast, no, though I've a finger in a lot of pies. But I've stuck mostly to what I know—anything to do with vehicles and transport.'

'What about the caravan site?'

'Oh, that and a couple of small hotels came with a garage chain I bought up last year. One of my brothers-in-law runs the leisure side as a subsidiary now.'

'So how come you were driving a truck full of vaccines through Africa?' she asked curiously.

He laughed. 'Oh, that was a busman's holiday,' he confessed. 'I don't very often get the chance to get behind the wheel of a truck these days, and I miss it. So when they rang and asked if we could help out, I jumped at it.'

'It was a very generous thing to do.'

He shrugged his wide shoulders in a gesture of dismissal. 'If pop-stars and sportsmen can do it, why not truck-drivers? I enjoyed it. Mind you,' he added grimly, 'I'd never have gone if I'd known what I was going to come back to.'

Penny lowered her eyes. He had every right to be angry—it had been wrong of Pete to go behind his back like that, especially when he was away risking his life in such a good cause. But she couldn't leave Pete undefended.

'I wish you'd give him a chance,' she pleaded. 'It's not his fault he's got no money—he tried, as you did, to start his own business, he and some of the other men from where he was working, after they were made redundant. But it didn't work out, and the only job he could find was working for you.'

'Were you telling me the truth about your parents?' he asked.

'Yes.'

'Oh—I'm sorry,' he said softly.

'It was . . . a long time ago,' she told him, responding to his sympathy. 'I was only twelve, and if Pete hadn't been prepared to look after me I'd have had to go to a foster-home or something. Mum was an only child, you see, and Dad's brother—my Uncle Ted—well, he had his own family, he couldn't have taken me on.'

'I see.'

'Pete was really good to me,' she went on

insistently. 'We had some great times together. And he worked really hard to make a go of that business—it wasn't his fault it went broke. So don't look down your nose at him just because he's only a caretaker on your caravan site—he's just as good as you are! And if you'd taken the trouble to get to know him, instead of going off at half-cock, you might have found out that he's just the right man for you daughter!'

He lifted a cynical eyebrow. 'You think so? Well, I should have the opportunity to get to know him soon, if we have a little luck, so I'll be able to see for myself if you're right.'

His tone clearly indicated that he seriously doubted it, and she lapsed into silence as the waiter brought their first course.

The food was excellent—a subtle blend of tastes and textures that would have tempted the weakest appetite. They spoke little as they ate; almost consciously she was locking every moment of this evening into her memory. She would never forget the way he looked tonight, the way his hard features were softened by the flickering glow of the candle, the way he smiled at her from time to time across the table.

Soon—probably tomorrow—this brief time with him would be over. She would be going back to London, to try to pick up the threads of her life. Maybe she'd see him again from time to time, if Pete and Clare stayed together—there might be a christening or two in a few years' time.

They finished the meal with a fragrant lotus-flower tea, served in pretty porcelain bowls decorated with Chinese dragons. Mike leaned back in his seat, regarding her with those level hazel eyes.

'So,' he began,'you know quite a lot about me now. Now it's your turn.'

She shrugged her slim shoulders, more than ever aware of the stark contrast between their two life-styles. 'Oh . . . there isn't much to tell. I come from Camberwell—not the most salubrious part of the world.' She smiled thinly. 'I live with my friend Lizzie—we've got a poky little bedsitter, just about big enough to swing a cat. But we were lucky to get it.'

'What sort of work do you do?'

'I'm unemployed—at the moment. I had a job in a shop, up West—just for the Christmas rush and the sales. Before that, I was stuffing envelopes for a firm in Rotherhithe, and before that . . . oh, I've been a tea-lady, I've even done some office cleaning.'

She listed her curriculum vitae with a certain defiant pride. No more than Pete did she enjoy being out of work, and she would try her hand at anything, enjoying the variety even if she didn't have the satisfaction of a career.

'Why don't you try to do something with your drawing?' he asked.

She shook her head with regret. 'I'd have loved to go to art college, but there wasn't enough money. I did try for a grant, but there's an awful lot of competition.'

'You don't need to go to art college,' he argued. 'Your talent is entirely natural and fresh. If the stuff I've seen is anything to go by, you could get yourself a job as an illustrator at the very least.'

'Oh, I wouldn't know where to start,' she demurred—it was something she had often thought of, but she had never had enough confidence to go ahead.

But Mike Wolfe was not the type to have any patience with that sort of diffidence. 'Rubbish!' he castigated her roundly. 'If you don't know, ask at the library or something. *Find out*. Don't just sit around on your backside dreaming of what you could have done.'

She smiled. 'Oh, maybe I'll think about it.'

'No—don't just think about it. Do it. What have you got to lose? You haven't even got a job at the moment.'

'I'll get another one,' she protested. 'I'm never out of work for long.'

'Doing what? Serving behind a counter in a shop? Filing, answering the telephone? You know there's more to life for you than that. Go out and grab it with both hands. So what if you get knocked back a few times? If you believe in yourself, you can do it.'

She stared at him, surprised at the hope he inspired in her. 'Do you really think I could?' she murmured, half to herself.

'I wouldn't have wasted my breath trying to persuade you if I didn't,' he countered brusquely.

That made her laugh. 'All right, I will,' she promised with sudden decision.

'Good. Well, then, would you like some more tea, or shall we go?'

'No more.' She lifted her eyes to meet his, a shy smile curving her soft mouth. 'Thank you—it was a lovely meal. I really enjoyed it,' she murmured.

His eyes smiled back at her, and she felt a warm glow begin, somewhere deep inside her, spreading through her whole body. The night was approaching fast, and she would have to make her choice. The waiter brought the bill, and then Mike helped her into her old duffle-coat, as gallantly as if it had been a creation of a top couture house.

The brief touch of his hands on her shoulders sent a jolt of electric current through her taut-strung nerve-fibres. She shook her hair out from the collar of her coat, struggling to steady her ragged breathing. She wasn't ready yet to show him how she felt, so she held herself very erect, her chin tilted at a proud angle as she preceded him out to the car.

Neither of them spoke as they drove back to the hotel. He parked the car in the garage at the side of the building, and they walked back to the front entrance together. The cinema further along the street was just closing, and young couples were strolling along, hand in hand or wrapped up in each other's arms.

Penny felt a painful twinge of jealousy—why couldn't life always be so simple? She ached to just reach out and take Mike's hand, or feel his arm around her, holding her close. She slanted a cautious glance up at him from beneath her lashes. He was walking along with his hands deep in his pockets, and it was impossible to read the thoughts behind his eyes.

The night-porter had just taken over from the receptionist, and he greeted Mike with recognition. 'Good evening, sir. Welcome back,'

he said. His glance turned briefly to Penny.
'Miss,' he acknowledged her discreetly. She felt
her cheeks tinge faintly pink as she guessed the
assumptions he was making.

'Good evening,' Mike responded pleasantly. 'I
booked in earlier in the day.'

'Of course, sir. Your suite is on the first floor.'
He handed over a key on a large blue tag. 'I hope
you'll find it satisfactory.'

'I'm sure I shall.'

'Would you like me to show you up, sir?'

'No, thank you—I can find the way,' Mike
responded, passing him a small tip. 'Penny . . .?'
He invited her to step into the lift ahead of him.

She couldn't look up at him; she kept her eyes
demurely lowered as they rode up to the first
floor, all her senses acutely tuned to his presence.
She felt as if she was trembling inside, and
wondered if he knew what she was thinking. He
was always so perceptive . . .

As the lift stopped, she risked a swift glance up
at him. He was very close, and suddenly the
awareness, never far below the surface, of the
kinetic tension created between his raw maleness
and her soft femininity flared like an arc light
between them.

But he turned away from her quickly, and
stepped out of the lift, striding along the corridor
at a brisk pace. She followed behind him, her
mind in a spin. In that fraction of a second in
the lift she had made her decision—but what
would he decide? Could the iron strength of his
will restrain those powerful desires for this one
last night?

She felt as if she were walking in a dream. The corridor had a strange, surreal atmosphere— long, straight, the lofty ceiling covered in dark blue art-deco wallpaper, the lights in their wall-sconces casting weird dancing shadows against the walls as they passed. Their footsteps made no sound on the dark blue carpet.

Mike stopped at one of the glass-panelled doors, and fitted the key into the lock. He held it open for her, and she stepped into a small lobby. He pushed open a door to her right, and flicked on the light.

She was in a bedroom. The same Edwardian décor as in the rest of the hotel prevailed, with a delicate green and pink William Morris wallpaper, mirrors in gilded frames on the walls—and a large double bed beneath an elegant rosewood tester.

Both their bags were at the foot of the bed—her scruffy old canvas holdall next to his well-used leather overnight bag. He glanced at them, a swift frown knitting his brows, and then walked through into the sitting-room of the suite.

A few seconds later he was back, a wry expression on his face. 'It seems that Frankie has been jumping to conclusions,' he remarked, a sardonic inflection in his voice.

She glanced up at him enquiringly.

'This is the only bedroom,' he informed her.

'Oh . . .' Her heart skidded, and began to race out of control.

But his hard mouth was set in a straight line.'Oh, indeed,' he mocked, reaching out to pull the eiderdown off the bed. 'It's a bit late at night to start messing around changing rooms now. It looks as if I'll be sleeping on the settee again.'

Penny drew a deep breath. 'You . . . don't have to,' she heard herself say.

He stared at her, his eyes cold.

'I bet you wouldn't sleep next door if you were with your secretary,' she threw at him in reckless challenge.

'What's that got to do with it?' he countered harshly.

He wasn't denying it, and a surge of jealous anger gripped her. 'You wouldn't, would you?' she demanded, tears stinging the backs of her eyes. 'I know about you and her—I could tell. I expect this was her way of telling you how sure and sophisticated she is,' she added bitterly, sweeping her hand to indicate the big double bed. 'She doesn't mind if you want to have a bit on the side now and then.'

He ran his hand back through his hair in an impatient gesture. 'Penny . . .'

'If you'd sleep with her, why not with me?' she pleaded, a passion stronger than pride reducing her to desperation. 'I know you want to. Last night——'

Something darkened in his eyes. 'Last night I thought you were . . . a woman of some experience,' he grated. 'I'm not the sort to go around casually deflowering virgins.'

'But every girl has to start somewhere,' she whispered, breathless as she recognised the taut stillness in him. She walked towards him slowly, her eyes holding his. She was close enough to touch him, but she held back, still afraid of his rejection. 'And they say it's always best . . . the first time . . . to choose someone who really knows what he's doing,' she added, feeling that slow blush spreading up over her cheeks.

'Who says that?' he demanded, his voice rough-edged.

She shrugged nervously. 'Oh . . . people, friends.' Suddenly she was afraid; she had started something very dangerous. But now there was no escape, she couldn't move—they were standing in a ring of fire that she had kindled herself.

His eyes slid over her slowly, deliberately subjecting her to the most insolent survey. 'And is that what you want?' he taunted harshly. 'To be taken like some cheap little tramp on a one-night-stand? To be just another notch on my belt? All right, then, come here.'

He grabbed her before she could escape, and jerked her roughly into his arms, and his mouth descended on hers in a kiss that was a ruthless assault. His lips crushed hers apart, and his tongue invaded with force into the sweet, moist valley of her mouth.

She struggled, startled and frightened by his unexpected savagery, but he was much too strong for her. It was just like in her dream—he was subduing her with almost contemptuous ease. And inevitably she began to respond, her resistance swept away by a tide of pure feminine submissiveness.

He had intended to teach her a lesson—she was sure he had only meant to frighten her, and then let her go. But as she yielded helplessly to his kiss the flames of his anger were engulfed in a fiercer fire, and his mouth broke from hers as he buried his face in her hair.

'God, Penny, I want you so much,' he groaned softly.

She wrapped her arms around his neck, hugging him tightly. 'And I want you, Mike,' she whispered. 'Please . . .'

He fell backwards on to the bed, taking her with him so that she lay along the length of his body, her soft dark curls tumbling over his face. 'I wish I'd never met you,' he growled, stroking his hand across her cheek. The tears welled into her eyes, and with a muttered curse against the fate that had put temptation into his way he slid his hand behind her head and drew her down to him.

Their mouths melted together in a kiss that was fired with all the hunger inside them both. Her senses were filled with him, with the warm strength of his arms around her, with the haunting male muskiness of his body. His sensuous tongue plundered every deep, secret corner of her mouth with an urgency that warned her he was no longer playing games.

His hand slid up beneath her woollen sweater to caress her bare back, and she broke from his kiss just long enough to pull the garment off over her head. Then he drew her back into his arms again, his mouth claiming hers in a kiss that was a heated exchange of desire.

He dealt quickly with the lacy scrap of her bra, tossing it aside, and then he rolled her over so that she lay back on the bed, half-crushed by his weight as his hand moulded and caressed the warm, arching ripeness of her breasts. His skilful touch was wreaking havoc on her senses, and she could hear her own breathing, ragged and impeded.

But he was taking his time, restraining the urgency of his own desire, leading her slowly and irrevocably down all the byways of seduction. His sensuous tongue swirled around the delicate shell of her ear, making her shiver with delight, and then his kisses moved on, down the vulnerable curve of her throat and into the sensitive hollows of her shoulder.

And then his head bent over her naked breasts, to kiss first one ripe rosebud nipple and then the other. She let go her breath in a long, shuddering sigh, quivering as his scalding tongue lapped sensuously around each hardened, sensitised peak, and the light nibbling of his teeth made her spine curl in ecstasy.

He laughed huskily at her wanton response. 'You're a sexy little thing,' he murmured. 'I must have been mad to think I could spend the night in the other room.'

She opened misted eyes to gaze up at him. 'Oh, Mike,' she whispered, 'I love you——'

But he silenced her even as she spoke, putting his fingers quickly across her lips. 'No, don't say it,' he warned roughly, shaking his head. 'This is just tonight—no more than that.'

She nodded dumbly, accepting his terms—what else could she do? Even though her heart was breaking, she knew that she could ask no more of him. Her had never made her any false promises, never pretended to be in love with her.

She wrapped her arms tightly around him, drawing herself close to him, fighting back the tears.

Her reward was a kiss that swept her beyond all shadows of regret into a land of pure erotic dreams. She surrendered everything he demanded and more, her tongue sparring playfully with his or teasing the corners of his lips, sending a tremor of arousal through his hard body.

With clumsy urgency she unfastened the buttons of his shirt, and peeled it back from his wide shoulders, shivering with a delicious response as the rough hair on his chest rasped against her tender breasts. They rolled on the bed, caught in the primeval drive of their own animal hunger.

He was impatient as he unsnapped her jeans, peeling them down over her slim thighs. She heeled off her canvas sneakers, not taking the time to unfasten the laces, and let them thud to the floor as he dragged the denim off over her feet.

But then he stopped, that deep chest moving on an intake of air as he gazed down at her, his eyes caressing every inch. 'You've got such dainty feet,' he murmured, lifting one to kiss her toes. 'You're dainty all over. Perfect.'

She smiled up at him happily. He found her attractive and that was all she needed.

But his eyes were troubled, and he shook his head. 'I shouldn't be doing this . . .' he murmured in self-reproach.

She reached for him pleadingly. 'It isn't wrong, Mike,' she whispered. 'I want you. Please don't stop.'

He came into her arms. 'I couldn't stop. God help me, Penny, wild horses couldn't drag me away from you now,' he groaned, his hot breath fanning her hair.

He stroked his hand over her body in a possessive gesture, lifting her in his arms as he slowly eased her tiny briefs down from her hips. He was murmuring to her softly, as if soothing a nervous kitten, but she wasn't afraid, and let him move her to his will.

His hand ran back in one smooth movement from her ankles, up over the silky inner flesh of her thighs, parting them slightly. A tremor of vulnerability ran through her, but she yielded in willing acquiescence as he sought the most intimate caresses. A small sob escaped her throat, and she buried her face in his shoulder, a honeyed tide of languid warmth flooding through her, starting from somewhere deep inside and spreading outward to every limb.

She clung to him, hearing her own voice begging in a strange, husky whisper, 'Mike . . . please . . .'

'It's all right,' he promised, his voice wrapping around her like smoke. 'We've got all night.'

She was barely breathing, lost in the magic of what he was doing to her. His touch was exquisite, finding the most sensitive spot and arousing her with infinite skill, until the pleasure was a delicious agony, building inside her to an impossible pitch.

And then at last he moved to lie above her, the powerful muscles in his shoulders bulging as he held his weight from crushing her. She wrapped her arms around him, sliding her hands over his smooth skin, moving her body beneath his in sensuous invitation.

'Don't be frightened,' he murmured softly, stroking the dark curls back from her face with an unsteady hand.

She shook her head. 'I'm not frightened,' she whispered, though her voice was shaking with mingled apprehension and anticipation.

The gentle touch of his fingers prepared the way, seeking out the deepest degree of intimacy, proving to her that there would be no pain to fear this time. She waited, her breath warm on her lips, loving him so much that she felt as though her heart would burst with it.

He took her with cherishing restraint, his hand on the pillow beside her clenching into a fist as he sustained the masterly effort of self-control. She felt the dampness of tears on her cheeks, but he kissed them away as he began to move inside her, slow and deep, building a rhythm that was irresistible, primeval.

She moved with him instinctively, offering herself to each thrust as his demand became more urgent, and he forgot to be gentle, buffeting her in a wild, hungry possession that was beyond all control. But she didn't care. She belonged to him totally, her first love and her last, and she wanted this moment to last forever.

The pleasure was mounting inside her, and she dug her fingers fiercely into his back, thrilling to the sheer masculine power of his body as he moved above her. They were both breathing raggedly, gasping for air, their skin slicked with sweat.

She had never dreamed it could be like this—nothing could have prepared her for this mindless bliss. She was drowning in it, her body on fire; the tension was too much to contain, and on a last strangled cry she let go, her mind spinning in free fall somewhere out beyond the bounds of the universe. With a last violent surge he came with her, unleashing the full force of his power over her until, with a final shudder, he fell into her arms, sated and exhausted as they drifted together in the ebbing afterglow of love.

CHAPTER EIGHT

IT WAS a long time before either of them moved. Penny felt nothing but the most complete satisfaction, but, acutely sensitive to the mood of the man beside her, she knew that he was troubled—and she knew that she was the cause of it. She had tempted him until he had betrayed his own code of honour.

She turned her head, and put a tremulous kiss on the lobe of his ear. 'Mike?' she said uncertainly. He shifted, opening his eyes to look down at her. She had to close her own eyes against the torment she saw there. 'Mike, I'm sorry,' she whispered painfully. 'I shouldn't have made you do it.'

He sighed heavily, but then the sigh turned to a laugh, low and husky, and he gathered her up in his arms again. 'Oh, Penny, you beautiful, adorable creature,' he murmured, covering her face with kisses. 'You didn't make me do anything I didn't want to do.'

She twisted close against him, twining her limbs around his. 'Really?' she breathed, her heart skipping.

'Really. I'd be plain stupid if I let myself regret anything we've done tonight.'

She wished silently that he would tell her that that was because he loved her, but she knew he wouldn't, and she wouldn't burden him with her love any more. She would just enjoy tonight—this one glorious night—and save her tears for tomorrow.

Her one regret was that he had taken precautions to see that she didn't get pregnant. Of course, he would be extra-careful, given his past history, and of course it was stupid to long for his baby—it was no picnic, she knew, being a single mum. But it would have been something of him, to cherish forever.

But there would be no baby. So she would just have to make do with her memories. And if they were all she had she would make sure that they were good ones—and make sure, too, that he would never forget tonight.

She began to move against him, the instincts of Eve teaching her all sorts of things she would never have dreamed of before. She found that he, too, had sensitive places—the lobe of his ear, the hollow of his shoulder—and her tongue swirled languorously over his skin, tasting its salty tang.

A powerful tremor of response ran through him. 'Hey, what are you doing?' he protested, half laughing in the agony of pleasure.

'Shut up,' she growled, pretending to be fierce. 'Just lie back and enjoy it.'

And he did, letting her caressing hands and hot mouth explore every inch of his hard-muscled body. She was delighted to discover how easily she could arouse him, and she used her new-found power to the full, gurgling with laughter as he groaned in ecstasy.

But then suddenly he caught her, and threw

her back on the bed. 'Right, then, miss,' he warned. 'This is where you pay for all that.'

She gasped at the touch of his hands on her sensitised skin. His clever fingers stroked over her breasts, teasing the ripe buds of her nipples, and she writhed in rapturous response, almost unable to endure the pleasure.

He laughed, low in his throat. 'You like this, don't you?' he taunted. 'Your breasts are perfect—good enough to eat.' His tongue swirled languorously around one berry-red peak, his teeth tugged at it gently, and she felt every nerve-fibre zinging with a million tiny sparks of electricity.

But now he was taking his time, torturing her, arousing her to fever pitch and then taking her impossibly beyond, into a land of pure erotic fantasy. His hand was stroking over her inner thigh in slow, sensuous circles, and she closed her eyes, weak with desire.

He went on until she was sobbing with need, begging him without restraint to take her. His mouth plundered her breasts, suckling deeply on each tender nipple, and then moved on to dust her smooth stomach with kisses, and at last sought the ultimate intimacy, firing a heat that made her gasp in shock as his rasping tongue lapped delicately over the exquisitely sensitive focus of all her responses.

It was a night without end. Their bodies merged and parted, loving and giving for hour upon hour, neither willing to waste a moment in sleep. But at last sheer exhaustion took over, and they lay tangled up in each other's arms as morning came.

Penny woke to find that she was alone in the big bed—only the rumpled sheets and the faintly musky aroma that lingered to haunt her told her that it hadn't been a dream. She turned her face into the pillow he had slept on, hugging it close to stifle her pain. Just one night—that was all she had asked for, and that was all she had got.

A few moments later she heard his voice in the next room; he was ordering breakfast from room-service. She scrambled out of bed, and ran into the bathroom to have a quick wash. Then she got dressed, pulling on her jeans and a pale blue lambswool jumper, and tried to brush her curls into some semblance of order. Then, taking a deep, steadying breath, she opened the door.

He was standing by the window, his hands deep in his trouser pockets. It was raining steadily, the drops running slowly down the pane. He didn't turn as she came into the room or acknowledge her presence in any way. She perched nervously on the edge of the settee until the waiter brought their breakfast.

She set out the cups, and glanced up uncertainly at his unresponsive back. 'Coffee?' she managed to say.

'Thank you.'

'Here you are, then.'

She set his cup down on the far corner of the table, and he did not meet her eyes as he came to fetch it. He picked up a croissant, and returned to his moody study of the rain-drenched street below. Penny ate, but the light roll was ashes in her mouth. She ached with misery. Her mind fumbled for a way to cross the gulf he had put between them, but it was unbridgeable.

Suddenly he stiffened, and swore softly. 'It's them!' he exclaimed. 'They're coming here!'

Penny ran to the window. It was the morning rush-hour, and down in the street the traffic was backed up in every direction around the traffic-lights outside the hotel. Pete was waiting on the traffic-island half-way across, his arm around the shoulders of a slim young woman with glossy dark hair. She was laughing up at him—they looked so happy, so much in love.

Mike's hand clenched into a fist, and he struck the window-frame. 'I'll swing for him,' he grated, his voice tense with fury. 'The bastard . . . I'll tear his throat out!'

'They're coming here,' she pointed out, resolutely calm in spite of his frightening anger. 'They must know we're here. They've come to see you, to try to sort things out with you. Won't you at least give them a chance?'

He stared at her for a moment as if she were a stranger, until the buzz of the telephone made him turn away. He picked it up. 'Yes . . . Send them up,' he spoke into it crisply, and then he sat down in the armchair opposite the door, staring at it fixedly, his burning gaze almost scorching the wood.

Penny heard their voices in the corridor outside, and crossed the room to open the door quickly. Pete stopped dead in his tracks. 'Penny?' He spoke her name incredulously. 'What are you doing here?'

'Come in, Pete, and we can both explain everything,' she said quietly.

He still had his arm around the shoulders of the dark-haired girl. 'This is Clare,' he introduced her with pride.

'I know.' She found herself smiling into a pair of bright, sparkling eyes.

'Hi—I've been dying to meet you,' the younger girl greeted her merrily. Pete's told me heaps about you.'

Penny hesitated. 'Well, I . . . I hope we'll have a chance to get to know each other,' she managed to say. She stepped aside. 'Your father's in there.'

Clare bit her lip, and moved past her. 'Dad?' she queried in an uncertain voice. Mike had risen to his feet, and for what seemed like an eternity the two stared at each other. Then suddenly she threw herself across the room, and swung herself around his neck. 'Oh, Dad!'

He lifted his daughter clean off her feet in an enormous bear-hug, and Penny was sure that it was a tear sparkling at the corner of his tight-clenched eyes. Her heart felt as though it would spill over. At long last he set the girl on her feet, but he still held her, glowering at Pete as he moved into the room and closed the door.

'Well?' His voice grated like steel gauze.

Clare detached herself from her father's grasp, and moved back to take Pete's arm. 'We're getting married, Dad,' she told him firmly. 'And there's nothing you can do to stop us.'

'Oh, can't I?' he growled. 'You're still a minor, my girl.'

'I know.' She sat down on the settee, drawing

Pete to sit beside her. Penny sank into one of the armchairs, feeling uncomfortably like an intruder, but unable to retreat from the scene. Mike was pacing impatiently around the room, but Clare didn't seem the least bit intimidated by him. 'I've got Mum's consent,' she announced.

Mike's head jerked round. '*What?*' he roared.

'Grandpa Tonini gave me her address,' she explained calmly.

'And who gave you his address—no, don't tell me. Your damned meddling grandmother.'

Clare nodded. 'She gave it to me ages ago, and I've been up to visit them.'

Mike finally sat down—he looked as if he'd been pole-axed. 'What else has been going on behind my back?' he enquired, glaring at her.

'Well, if you weren't so unreasonable, it wouldn't have been necessary,' she told him, unruffled. 'After all, even though you didn't get on with them, they're just as much my grandparents as Nanna is.'

He stared at her in stunned silence.

'I went to see Mum last week, and she was quite happy to give me her consent.'

'I just bet she was,' growled Mike. 'After all these years—she's finally got her revenge.'

'It's perfectly legal, sir,' put in Pete. 'You've never divorced your wife, and in fact you've not even got legal custody of Clare, so she's perfectly entitled to give her consent.'

'Damn you!' cursed Mike fiercely. 'I never divorced her because I was afraid of fighting her for custody, in case I lost.' He cast a swift glance at Penny's ashen face, and Pete, noticing the interaction between them, frowned. 'So you think you've got me over a barrel?' Mike demanded harshly. 'How much do you want to leave my daughter alone?'

The two men faced each other like feral dogs, spoiling for a fight. 'I don't want a penny of your money,' Pete grated through clenched teeth.

Mike laughed unpleasantly. 'Ten thousand? Twenty? Come on, name your price,' he jeered.

'I told you, I won't touch a brass farthing,' repeated Pete, ice-cold rage burning in his handsome face. Penny's nails were digging into her palms as she watched them, terrified that they were about to come to blows.

'Good!' snapped Mike. 'Because you won't get your hands on a groat. I'll cut her off—that's the end of her allowance. And I've got plenty of nieces and nephews to put in my will. You won't even get a sniff of it, not if you wait fifty years!'

'That's exactly what I want,' Pete returned with all the firm determination that Penny knew so well. 'I don't want to live off my wife's money. I can support her myself—maybe not in the way she's used to, but I'll do everything I can to make her happy. I won't mind you giving her presents now and then, within reason—and your grandchildren too, of course——'

'Grandchildren?' exploded Mike, rising to his feet again. 'I should have anticipated that, I suppose. How soon can I expect the patter of tiny feet?'

'In about five years,' Clare informed him with dignity. 'We don't want to rush it—I'm only young yet.' Mike made some incoherent noise in his throat, and strode over to stare out of the window again. 'And I do wish you'd listen, Dad, instead of pacing about like some great big grizzly bear. Pete's every bit as Victorian as you are.' Her eyes danced as she gazed up warmly at her beloved. 'He's insisted we have separate rooms until after we're married.'

Mike started guiltily, and again Pete glanced from him to Penny, and then around the room, swiftly noting the layout—only one bedroom. His eyes flashed with knowing anger.

'We've got it all worked out,' Clare went on, blissfully innocent of the dark undercurrents that were flowing counter to her own all-absorbing romance. 'We're going to move down to Torquay, and get jobs in a hotel. We're going to save as hard as we can, and learn everything about the hotel business, and then in a couple of years we're going to start up a small place of our own.'

Mike sat down again abruptly, staring at his daughter as if seeing her for the first time. 'Is that what you want?' he asked after a long while. 'A life of drudgery and hard work?'

She nodded confidently. 'You worked your way up from nothing, Dad,' she reminded him. 'We can do the same. And we're in love—I know you think I'm much too young, and Pete agreed with you at first. He wanted us to wait. But when you slammed the phone down on him, and had him thrown out of your office, and then you threatened to send me to America, he realised that this was the only way. It's going to work, Dad. Not like you and my mother. We'll make it work.'

'I'm sorry it had to be this way, sir,' added Pete

respectfully. 'I wanted to talk to you, convince you that my intentions were honourable——'

'Oh, don't talk to me about honourable intentions!' snapped Mike, leaning back in his chair and closing his eyes as if he wanted to block out the whole scene from his mind.

'I'm sorry, sir, but I think I must,' Pete went on with quiet insistence. 'I hope I've demonstrated mine towards your daughter, and now I have to ask about yours towards my sister.'

A surge of horror brought Penny to her feet. 'Pete, *no*,' she begged urgently. 'Don't you dare.' Spinning round, she ran into the bedroom, slamming the door shut behind her and leaning against it.

It was still raining, and with a kind of hopeless despair in her heart she walked over to the window and leaned her forehead against the cool glass. The raindrops were running down the pane and mingling with each other, like the tears she couldn't shed.

In a little while they would finish their discussion next door, and she would say goodbye to Mike—maybe he would take her to Pierhead to board the coach. And nothing would ever be the same again—there would be nothing but endless rainy days. Colours would never seem as bright, tastes and perfumes never as rich. And no man would ever make her feel the way he had. But at least she had one night, to treasure and remember forever.

Some time later, the door opened behind her, but she didn't turn. She heard him cross the room towards her, but he stopped about a foot away, not touching her. She could see a faint image of his face in the rain-lashed window.

'They've gone,' he said at last, in a voice that was drained of all emotion.

She wanted to say something, but her brain wouldn't function. It was as if she was out there in the cold, on the other side of the glass, as dim and unreal as her own reflection.

'They saw the car last night—Clare knew I'd been staying here. She thought I'd got the information out of her grandmother—she should have known better.' He laughed in grim self-mockery. 'There seems to have been quite a conspiracy going on behind my back.'

He drew a long breath, and then went on, 'They've agreed to postpone the wedding for six months, until her eighteenth birthday. If they're both still of the same mind then, I'll give them my blessing. Fortunately Clare doesn't seem so enamoured of her mother that she's insisting on inviting her or her family to the wedding,' he added drily.

Still Penny said nothing.

'In the meantime, your brother's coming to work for me, so that I can see what he's made of. He'll start at one of the hotels in Birmingham—at the bottom. If he proves himself—well, I'll see. They still seem quite keen on this idea of theirs, to set up on their own—I don't think they realise what a struggle it's likely to be ... Or maybe they do,' he mused, shrugging his shoulders.

He laughed with wry self-mockery. 'I still can't get used to it,' he admitted. 'All of a sudden she's a young woman. But she certainly seems to know her own mind, and . . . he seems steady enough. Maybe it'll work out all right.' He moved away from her to sit down on the edge of the bed.

She turned, forcing a smile. 'I hope it will,' she managed to say. 'I think . . . you and Pete will get on great when you get to know each other.'

'Maybe,' he conceded doubtfully.

She walked round the bed to fetch her bag from the cupboard in the lobby, and began to collect up the things she had left in the bathroom, returning to the bedroom for the oddments on the dressing-table. He was watching her steadily, not saying anything. Finally she zipped up the bag, and picked up her duffle-coat from the chair where she had left it.

'Well, that's it,' she announced, turning to face him bravely.

This time it was he who couldn't meet her eyes. 'Yes. I'll run you home,' he offered gruffly.

'Oh, no,' she protested at once. 'That isn't necessary. I had a return coach ticket from Wrexham—I'm sure I can change it.'

'I'll run you home,' he repeated firmly, picking up her bag. 'It's the least I can do.'

She capitulated without any further argument. Her dream was over, and all she had to do now was pick up the pieces.

Six months. It seemed incredible that it could have been so long—it had gone by so quickly. Penny gazed out of the window as the train rushed by the houses and industrial estates of Birmingham. She was on her way to Pete and Clare's wedding.

She had been right about her brother and his young love—they were very well matched. She brought him lightness and laughter, he brought her the steadiness to balance her exuberance. And he had proved himself to Mike, too—after slaving for several months as a lowly assistant porter at one of Mike's hotels in Birmingham, he had recently been promoted to a much more important position in the leisure subsidiary run by Mike's brother-in-law.

In return, Mike had kept his promise. It was to be a grand wedding, to judge by Clare's vivid descriptions—several hundred guests, a marquee in the garden of Mike's riverside house, entertainment until after midnight from two bands, a sumptuous four-tier cake. And his wedding present to them was the deposit on a house of their own.

And as for Mike . . . Well, he had finally divorced his wife, and from Clare's reports was making the most of his new-found freedom.

'I expect it's a relief to him, now I'm off his hands,' she had mused the last time they had met, innocently unaware that Penny had any special interest in the matter. 'All I hope is that if he does decide to get married again, he doesn't pick any of the current bunch. That Francine, for instance—his secretary. She's been trying to get her claws into him for years, but I can't say I like her very much.'

Pete had laughed, slanting a searching gaze at Penny's face. 'I'm sure your dad can take care of himself,' he had advised her. 'He's not in much danger of being trapped by any scheming little gold-digger.'

'I hope you're right,' Clare had conceded. 'I don't fancy being saddled with a wicked stepmother!'

Penny bit her lip. It was going to be difficult to meet him again—she hadn't seen him since he had dropped her outside the tall old house in south London, and she had stood on the pavement watching him drive away.

She wasn't sure how she felt—all she knew was that she hadn't met anyone else who could arouse even an echo of the excitement she had felt with him. It hadn't been easy to pick up the pieces, but she had survived somehow, living at first from day to day.

Strangely, it had been Ken whom she had confided in, rather than Lizzie. He had been comforting, accepting that there was no more between them now than friendship. In fact, he had readily turned his attention to Lizzie, and the two of them were growing increasingly cosy.

And Penny had kept the promise she had made to Mike in the Chinese restaurant, sending off a batch of her best drawings to an agent, whose name she had found in a book in the library. The first one she had picked hadn't been interested, but she had tried again, and the second had been much more encouraging.

So far she had had only a couple of very small commissions, but there were several more in the pipeline, including the possibility of a set of Get Well cards featuring a cast of fluffy rabbits with droopy ears, confined to hospital beds, complete with thermometers and hot-water bottles.

The train drew into Walsall station, and Penny picked up her bag and stepped down on to the platform. Clare was meeting her, and they were going to do a bit of last-minute shopping—it was just two days to the wedding. She was waiting at the ticket-gate, and she bobbed up on tiptoe, waving, as soon as she saw Penny.

There was a man beside her . . . Penny's heart thudded alarmingly. Tall, ruggedly built . . . But as she saw his face clearly she realised that it wasn't Mike. He was so like him, he must be one of his younger brothers—there were three of them, and two sisters, and they all worked for him, as did his in-laws and several of his cousins. "'Blood's thicker than water.'" Pete had quoted him—she could almost hear him say it.

'Penny!' Clare greeted her with her usual open friendliness. 'Hi—lovely to see you. Good journey? This is my Uncle Chris—he's been dying to meet you.'

'Hey, less of the 'Uncle', young lady—I'm only seven years older than you.' The voice, though pleasant in its way, was a disappointment to Penny—there was no trace of any fascinating Geordie brogue. And though he was undeniably good-looking, his face was rather . . . boyish. The eyes weren't quite right, either.

He held out one large paw. 'But she's right,' he confided, turning on a smile that would have had most women swooning, 'I've heard so much about you—I've been looking forward to meeting you very much. And you're not a disappointment.' His gaze swept over her in undisguised approval. 'Even your photos don't do you justice.'

Penny returned him a friendly smile. 'Thank you. And I've heard a lot about you, too.'

'Oh? Not the truth, I hope?' he teased mischievously.

They all laughed. 'Come on,' urged Clare, linking arms with her in a sisterly fashion. 'Don't take any notice of him—I only brought him along to carry the parcels.'

'Hey!' he protested, laughing good-naturedly.

'So make yourself useful,' Clare added to him over her shoulder, 'and carry Penny's bag.'

It proved to be a lively shopping expedition. Chris kept them both in fits of laughter, and Penny found herself liking him a lot. He was so like Mike to look at—sometimes, if she just squinted her eyes a little, she could almost pretend . . .

But that was just foolish. He *wasn't* Mike. Maybe if she was meeting Mike for the first time now, they could have got to know each other in this relaxed, enjoyable way. But it could never be like that now, she reminded herself wistfully. They could never turn back the hands of time.

It was almost five o'clock by the time they drew up outside Pete and Clare's new house. It was a narrow Victorian terrace, but Clare couldn't have been more proud of it if it had been a palace. They had been doing it up for a month, working on it in every spare moment they had.

The four dogs came bounding out of the kitchen to greet them as Clare opened the door. Penny stroked their heads and tickled their ears as they wagged their tails joyously. 'It's worse than the zoo in here,' grumbled Chris, grinning as he dumped Clare's parcels on the hall table.

'Oh, go and put the kettle on,' she scolded him cheerfully. 'Well?' she added to Penny. 'What do you think of it now it's nearly finished?'

Penny gazed around with interest—the last time she had visited, it had been a bare shell, but the couple had worked hard. 'It's lovely,' she approved warmly.

'Good—I'm glad you like it. Dad wanted to buy us a big house for a wedding present, but Pete wouldn't let him—he insisted we'd take out a mortgage ourselves. They had a bit of a row about it, actually, but Dad gave way in the end. Do you know, I think he likes Pete more because of the way he stands up to him—he's the only one that does, apart from me. Oh, there's Pete now!'

She ran to the front gate, and threw herself into his arms. He put down his briefcase and swung her up in the air. 'Hello, my sunshine,' he greeted her with deep affection, giving her a welcoming kiss.

Chris, standing in the doorway of the sitting-room, chuckled with laughter. 'Well, if you two are going to start canoodling,' he teased, 'I'm going home.'

'Oh, wait,' protested Clare quickly. 'You've got to give me a lift.' She ran to fetch her handbag. 'Don't be late,' she reminded Pete and Penny. 'Eight o'clock.' They were to dine with the whole family, at a restaurant Mike owned nearby.

'We won't be late,' Pete promised her, giving her a parting hug.

Chris turned to Penny. 'Well, I'll see you this

evening, then,' he said, turning on that attractive Wolfe smile. 'I'll be looking forward to it.'

She returned his smile, though wary of that glint of special warmth in his brown eyes. 'Yes—tonight,' she murmured, stepping back before he could think of kissing her goodbye.

Pete slanted a teasing smile at her as the other two drove away. 'Well you seem to have made a conquest already,' he commented with brotherly amusement.

'Oh . . . he's very nice,' she responded lightly.

'Yes. They're all very nice. I'm sorry you're having the whole Wolfe-pack thrust upon you at once tonight, but I thought it was a good opportunity for you to get to know them.'

'I'm looking forward to it,' she assured him. 'And it's better than seeing them all for the first time on Saturday—at least I'll know some of the faces.'

'Yes.' He hesitated. 'And . . . what about Mike? You don't mind seeing him again?'

She shrugged her slim shoulders in a feint of indifference. 'No, of course not,' she insisted. 'Why should I mind?'

'Good. I wondered, you know—in Liverpool.'

She managed a laugh. 'Oh, don't be silly. I did quite fancy him—you've got to admit, he's very attractive. But there was never anything serious about it.'

He didn't look quite convinced, but he didn't pursue the matter any further, and soon she was able to make the excuse that she needed to start getting ready, thus avoiding any risk of further discussion.

CHAPTER NINE

THE restaurant was in Aldridge—not so long ago a leafy village, and still retaining much of its charm, though the vast urban sprawl of the West Midlands had almost engulfed it. The restaurant was on a corner, beside a row of shops—it looked as if it had been converted from a pub. It was clearly very popular, if the number of expensive cars parked in front of it on a Thursday night was any indication.

The knot of nervous tension that had been building up inside Penny all day—all week—was making her feel almost physically sick. Fortunately Pete seemed to assume it was due to her nervousness at meeting so many strangers all at once—or at least, if he thought it was due to anything else he didn't ask any questions.

There was a small bar in the foyer, and the family were all gathered there in a chatting, laughing group. One swift glance told her that Mike hadn't yet arrived, and she let go her breath in a silent sigh, aware that her palms were moist with sweat.

Chris was at her side at once, his brown eyes alight with warm approval. 'Hi—you look fabulous,' he murmured, leaning a little closer than she liked.

She responded with a small smile. She had

been anxious that her dress would show its cheap price-tag, even though she had taken off the floppy bow at the neckline and replaced it with an old cameo brooch that had been her mother's. It was a simple style, in a soft dusky pink that suited her, the fine jersey fabric skimming her slender figure and flirting around her knees.

'Come and meet the Wolfe-pack,' urged Chris, dropping a possessive arm around her shoulders and drawing her forward. 'This is my Mum.'

The matriarch of the family was in her fifties. She had probably never been a beauty, but there was considerable character in her strong-boned face, and her gaze was very direct. 'Hello, my dear,' she greeted Penny warmly. 'I'm so glad to meet you at last. My granddaughter never stops talking about you—and neither, since this afternoon, has my son,' she added, slanting her youngest a twinkling glance.

Penny felt her cheeks flush faintly pink. She had recognised this afternoon that Chris was attracted to her, but she hadn't expected him to make it quite so blatantly obvious in front of his family. She liked him, of course, but . . . it was no more than that. That zing of excitement she had felt the first time she had seen Mike just wasn't there with his youngest brother.

She managed to attend to the rest of the introductions just enough to remember who was who. Mike's stepfather, George, was an amiable man, clearly held in great affection by the family he had taken on. All the Wolfe men, and their two sisters, bore a striking family resemblance—*en masse* they could have been quite overwhelming if they hadn't all been so friendly and welcoming.

But she was on edge, her heart fluttering, her eyes constantly flickering towards the door. It opened once or twice, making her flinch, but each time it was someone else. It was Clare who finally voiced the question that was burning in her brain.

'Where's Dad?' she asked of everyone in general. 'He's very late—he *is* coming, isn't he?'

'He said he'd be here,' one of her uncles reassured her. 'He was tied up with that Japanese trade delegation when I left.'

'He's not bringing Francine, is he?' enquired Clare, wrinkling her pretty nose in distaste.

'I don't know who he's bringing.'

'Well, if he's not here soon, we'd better sit down,' she declared, her firm insistence reminiscent of her father.

But suddenly there was a kind of sprucing up among the already immaculate staff, and someone said, 'No, here he is now.'

Penny could see him in the mirror behind the bar without turning round. He walked in, a presence that was instantly commanding without the least apparent effort. Not one line of his face had changed—it was still exactly as it had been etched into her memory six months ago. He was wearing a dark suit that subtly underlined that hint of masculine power, but his eyes were smiling as he apologised for his lateness.

He hadn't brought his secretary—he was with a tall, elegant redhead, beautifully dressed and exuding sophistication. Clearly she was a regular girlfriend, because she needed no introduction to the family, greeting them all with a cool, self-assured smile.

He didn't appear to notice Penny at once, and she was glad of the brief respite to gather a little composure, so that when he turned to her at last she was able to meet his eyes without evasion. 'Hello, Penny,' he said, offering her his hand in a gesture of formal politeness. 'Nice to see you again. How have you been keeping?'

'Oh—very well, thank you.' Would he notice the slight tremor in her voice, the tremble of her fingers as she placed them briefly in his?

He turned to the woman at his side. 'Diane, this is Penny,' he told her. 'Pete's sister.'

She found herself the subject of a faintly condescending appraisal, and was suddenly aware again of the cheapness of her dress beside this woman's chic black silk suit. 'How do you do?' she murmured uneasily.

'Good evening,' the older woman responded, her tone only just on the polite side of boredom. She turned back at once to Mike, her hand possessively on his arm. 'By the way, darling, you won't forget you've promised to come and look over those cars for me tomorrow, will you? I've almost decided on the Lamborghini, but the Ferrari's so beautiful—I need you to help me make up my mind.'

'"I need you to help me make up my mind",' mimicked Clare with wicked sarcasm as the pair drew away. 'I certainly hope he isn't bringing *her* to the wedding! I'd rather have Frankie.'

'Now, Clare,' her grandmother scolded her. 'You know it isn't any of your business who your father chooses to go out with.' But her expression indicated that she was inclined to agree.

Now that everyone had arrived, it was time to take their places for dinner. Chris was still close at Penny's side as they made their way through the restaurant. It was busy, but the tables were not packed too closely together, and the décor—a blend of modern and art-deco, with a colour scheme of peach and cream—gave it an airy, spacious feel.

To her relief, Penny found herself seated at the far end of the table from Mike. Chris had taken the seat beside her, and handed her the menu, sharing it with her and helping her make her selection from the mouth-watering choice. She felt a little guilty for encouraging him in this way, but she was confident that there was little danger of her doing any permanent damage to his heart.

The food was excellent, but it was wasted on Penny. All the time she was aware of Mike, at the far end of the table. He didn't glance her way again—he was chatting to the others about the trade delegation, teasing Clare about the lavish arrangements for the wedding, and also—it was impossible not to notice—sharing a few intimate words with his girlfriend.

She tried to flirt with Chris, but her heart felt as flat as left-over champagne. She couldn't stop herself covertly watching the couple at the other end of the table, envying the beautiful redhead that low, musical laugh and the way she moved her hands gracefully as she spoke.

Well, she had wondered whether, seeing Mike again after all this time, she would still feel the same—or whether, as he had said, she would find that it had been after all just a passing infatuation. And now she knew—nothing had changed. She was still in love with him.

And he still wasn't in love with her. She was just a girl he had once known, for whom he had felt a fleeting desire. But that desire had been satisfied, long ago, and now that night they had spent together was for him just a distant memory.

But for her it would never be forgotten. It would live in her mind as vividly as if it had been only yesterday. She had been held in those arms, those firm lips had kissed hers, those strong male hands had caressed her body . . .

Almost as if he was aware of her thoughts, he glanced along the table and caught her eye. She felt as if her heart had stopped beating, trapped again in the spell of his steady gaze. He didn't smile, he made no acknowledgement—he just looked at her.

'. . . Penny'll be bound to, won't you, Penny?' She blinked, and turned quickly back to Chris. 'You'll come on to a club after this, won't you?' he asked, smiling in confidence of her agreement.

'Oh . . . Yes, of course, I'd love to,' she responded unthinkingly.

'Good. I bet you're a fantastic dancer,' he added, leaning intimately close to her again as he refilled her wine-glass. 'I can't wait to get you out on the floor.' There was a mischievous glint in his eyes that implied that that wasn't all he couldn't wait to do.

She smiled up at him, grateful for his flattering attention as a balm to her wounded spirit. 'I shall

probably tread all over your toes,' she warned
him teasingly.

He laughed. 'In that case I shall just have to
pick you up in my arms,' he countered.

Penny's smile wavered, but she held it firmly
in place. He was beginning to make quite
definitely sexual overtones, and it really wasn't
fair of her to raise his expectations in this way.
But she needed him as a kind of shield to hide
from Mike the pain in her heart. And, after all,
it was only for a couple of days.

'Who else is coming?' she asked, a little
belatedly.

'Pete and Clare, and Steve and Mo, and Dave
and Linda. Anyone else?' he enquired around the
table. 'How about you, Mike?'

Mike shook his head, laughing. 'Count me out
tonight,' he demurred.

Beside him, Diane smiled in satisfaction, and
Penny felt a painful twist of jealousy in her heart.
Such a thoroughbred creature would be
supremely out of place in a noisy discotheque.
She could well imagine the way the evening
would end for her and Mike.

He would take her home—she probably lived
in some smart detached house on the edge of
town. She would discreetly invite him in for coffee—fresh-ground, of course, with cream—and
they would drink it in her elegant drawing-room,
listening to something smooth and sophisticated
on the stereo. She would kick off her shoes—a
provocative little touch of sexiness, that—and invite him to dance . . .

The image was so vivid that she almost felt as

though she were a fly on the wall, watching the slow seduction. With an effort of will she dismissed the tormenting vision from her mind and turned to Chris again, flirting with him so vivaciously that several of the family noticed, and smiled in amused understanding.

It was late when they left the restaurant. Penny was beginning to have doubts about the wisdom of going on to the disco with Chris—but, after all, there would be plenty of people to chaperon them. And, besides, the only alternative was to go home to bed and lie awake thinking of Mike.

As she let Chris hand her into the back of Pete's car, she couldn't resist a brief glance towards the Aston Martin. Diane was settling herself into the leather seat where she had once sat herself, and she smiled up at Mike as he held the door for her, saying something that made him laugh and look across to where the noisy group were getting ready to set off to the disco.

'Have a good time,' he called.

'We will!' responded Chris with a casual wave of his hand as he climbed in beside Penny. He dropped his arm around her shoulders and drew her close, and she didn't resist. She just wanted to blank out all thoughts of Mike, and maybe his younger brother could help her do that.

But it didn't work. All the spinning lights and pounding music in the crowded disco couldn't drown out the whisper of her memories. She really tried hard to enjoy herself, dancing with Chris, letting him hold her closer as the night wore on and the music slowed.

But she couldn't get Mike out of her mind. All

the time she was thinking about him, wishing he were the one here with her now. When Chris kissed her, she closed her eyes and let herself believe that it was Mike. Leaning her cheek against Chris's hard chest, his hand stroking her hair, she almost whispered Mike's name.

It was after two o'clock when they finally left the disco. All the way home she nestled in Chris's arms in the back of the car, letting him kiss her and murmur flattering words in her ear. In the darkness, he couldn't see the tears that filled her eyes, unshed. She was beginning to hate herself for using him like this, but she didn't have the strength to stop what was happening—all her emotional energy was being wasted in aching for Mike.

The car drew to a halt, and Pete half turned in the driver's seat. 'Hey, break it up, you two,' he castigated them cheerfully. 'We're home.'

Chris let her go reluctantly, with a last lingering kiss. 'See you Saturday,' he murmured as he climbed out of the car with Clare.

'Yes . . .' They were at Mike's house, and she gazed up at it in a hungry curiosity. It was screened by a row of tall trees, and all she could see was a frontage of weathered stone, pale yellow in the moonlight, one wall clad with ivy. There was no sign of Mike's car—but maybe it was in the garage. Maybe.

'It . . . looks a nice house,' she murmured, glancing back as they drove away.

'Mmm,' agreed Pete, noticing no sign of strain in her voice. 'It used to be a water-mill. It was almost derelict when he bought it, but he's done a lot to it—made it very nice. Well, you'll see it on Saturday.'

Penny had already heard from Clare every detail of the arrangements: about the large marquee that was being erected on the lawn next to the house, beside the river; about the two bands that had been engaged to play, one in the afternoon, the other far into the evening; about the spectacular cake and the huge guest-list.

'It sounds as if it's going to be quite a wedding,' she mused. 'Don't you mind it—all the fuss, I mean?'

Pete smiled. 'It doesn't make the least scrap of difference to me and Clare,' he told her contentedly. 'We're happy to go along with it—after all, it's something you only do once in your lifetime, so why not make a real splash of it? And her grandmother is loving every minute of it—we couldn't disappoint her by just slipping away quietly to a register office.'

She gave his arm an impulsive squeeze. 'You know, I'm so happy for you,' she said. 'You're a perfect couple.'

'Oh, there's no such thing as that,' he demurred with a laugh. 'Everyone has to work at it. But if we're just half as happy as our mum and dad were, I'll be satisfied.'

Penny nodded. 'It's a shame they can't be here to see it,' she murmured wistfully.

He squeezed her hand. 'Don't be sad,' he urged. 'They wouldn't want that.'

'No.' She managed a bright smile. 'I'm looking forward to it. Rather you than me, though.' He slanted her an enquiring glance. 'If I ever get married, *I* shall just slip away to a register office, and tell everyone about it afterwards.'

He laughed again.'Don't you want a big white wedding, with all the trimmings?' he teased.

'No, I don't!' She didn't add that she couldn't imagine herself ever getting married, not now. A fleeting fantasy image had slipped into her mind, unbidden, of herself and Mike, their two pairs of hands folded up in each other, gazing into each other's eyes as they recited their wedding vows. If she couldn't have that, she didn't want anything else.

She had planned to spend the Friday quietly with Pete, but Chris found an excuse to come over, and she succumbed to his cajoling to go out with him instead. They drove a little way up the motorway and went to a giant amusement park.

It wasn't the sort of place she would have chosen to go to—it was bright and noisy, and packed with holiday crowds, and each ride was more terrifying than the last. But at least it stopped her thinking about Mike for a few hours.

But this flirtation with Chris was becoming a bit too much to handle, and it was a relief to be spared from spending the entire evening in his company, as she had feared, by his determination to fulfil the time-honoured duty of best man—namely, to take the bridegroom out and get him comprehensively drunk.

'But I'll be back later,' he said quietly to Penny as he bid her goodbye at the door. 'I'm staying here tonight.'

There was a meaningful gleam in his eyes, and

she realised with a stab of guilty alarm that she had probably led him on a bit too far. She could only hope that, even if he came home a little the worse for drink, he would still remember his manners.

Sitting on her own, with the dogs at her feet, brought back so many memories of those few precious days in Wales. They seemed now like some impossible dream. Maybe she was lucky that just once in her life, even for so short a time, she had known such a pure intensity of feeling. Some people never had that.

Now she must accept that it was never going to come again, that she would never meet another man like Mike, and settle herself to a life alone, developing her new career. It would be better to preserve that one perfect memory than to tarnish it by searching among cheap imitations.

There was only tomorrow to get through—the wedding. After that she could go back to London again, and it would probably be another six months, or even longer, before she saw Mike again. And time would heal the wounds—wouldn't it?

It was the small hours of the morning when at last the sound of a taxi drawing up outside told her that the revellers had returned. She slipped out of bed, put on her dressing-gown, and went to the top of the stairs. There was a good deal of muffled noise coming from the porch—there must be more than just the two of them. She was just going down to let them in when the key found the lock, and the door opened.

Pete crept in, looking more rumpled than she had ever seen him, and Chris was in an even worse state. Behind him, the other male members of the Wolfe-pack crowded in, all looking as if they had had an exceptionally good time. And at the back, a little more sober than the others, was Mike.

'Shh,' whispered Pete. 'I don't want to wake my sister.'

'I'm already awake,' she informed him, smiling down on them all with an amused tolerance. 'Why don't you all go into the sitting-room, and I'll make you some coffee—black!'

At the sound of her voice, Chris lifted his head and smiled blearily up at her. 'Hello, Penny,' he greeted her. 'Isn't she pretty? You never told me she was so pretty, Pete.'

'Yes, I did—I'm sure I did,' argued Pete. 'And you saw her photograph—that's why you insisted on going with Clare to meet her off the train.'

'Oh . . . yes, I did, didn't I?' he agreed, after giving the matter a moment's careful consideration. 'But her photograph doesn't do her justice, you know.'

'I think you'd better sit down before you fall down,' Mike advised him drily, ushering them all into the sitting-room. As Penny hesitated on the stairs, he glanced up at her, his lopsided smile telling her that he was not quite as sober as he appeared. 'I'm sorry—I'm afraid we've all had a little too much to drink,' he told her unnecessarily.

'Quite.' Seeing him standing there, his hands in his pockets as he tried not to sway, made her long to run down and throw her arms around him. For once he wasn't quite in control. 'I'll put the kettle on,' she added unsteadily, stepping down to the hall.

He didn't move to let her pass him—he just stood there looking down at her with those deep hazel eyes she had loved so well. 'How have you been, Penny?' he enquired, his voice low and soft.

'You asked me that before,' she reminded him, making a brave effort to smile. 'I'm fine.'

'Good. Er . . . Clare told me about your drawing,' he went on conversationally.

'Oh . . .' She shrugged, struggling to retain a semblance of composure. 'Yes, it's going quite well. I've done some illustrations for a book of children's poetry, and I've had a couple of sketches accepted for a calendar, and with a bit of luck I'll be doing a set of greetings cards next. I'm not exactly making a fortune, but . . . I'm working on it.'

'I'm glad,' he said. 'I knew you had it in you.'

'Thank you.' She was gazing up at him, feeling the tug of that powerful magnetic force he exerted. All she wanted to do was reach out and touch him . . .

'Ah, there you are.' Chris lurched into the hall and swung her boisterously into his arms. 'Where have you been all my life?' he demanded, nuzzling into the hollow of her shoulder. 'I never thought I'd find a girl like you.'

'Chris—careful! You'll have me on the floor,' she protested, laughing with embarrassment. When she looked up, Mike had turned away and followed the others into the sitting-room. She

didn't know whether to be angry with Chris for
interrupting, or relieved that he had saved her
from making an utter fool of herself.

'I want you, Penny,' he was mumbling thickly,
trying to get his hands inside her dressing-gown.
'Come on, let's go up to bed.'

He tried to drag her towards the stairs, but she
stopped him firmly. 'No,' she insisted. 'Come on,
Chris, do as Mike said. Sit down before you fall
down.'

She finally managed to coax him into the
sitting-room, and deposited him in an armchair,
her cheeks pink as she realised that in their tussle
her dressing-gown had fallen open. She
refastened it quickly, hoping no one had noticed,
and escaped to make the coffee.

By the time she returned with the tray of cups,
Chris had fallen asleep, sprawled in an armchair.
The others had turned on the television, and were
watching a late-night horror movie, hooting with
laughter at the gruesome special effects.

She handed out the coffee, managing some sort
of smile for Mike as she passed him his cup and
quickly moving on to his second brother, Doug.
They were all in buoyant spirits, joking and
laughing, thanking her profusely for the coffee
and voting her a good sport for taking their
drunken disturbance of her sleep in such good
part. She teased them in return, warmed by their
friendly acceptance of her.

It took three of them to get Chris into bed, and
Pete crashed out beside him, still in his shirt. 'Just
get me to the church on time,' he mumbled,
groaning as his future brothers-in-law gleefully

took up the refrain, singing as they trundled down the stairs.

There was already a pale glimmer of dawn in the sky when they finally piled out to the taxi that had been waiting for them, clocking up a small fortune on the meter, all that time. Penny went to the door to wave goodbye. On the doorstep, Mike turned and smiled down at her.

'Well, goodnight—or rather good morning,' he corrected himself wryly. 'I'm sorry we woke you up.'

'That's all right,' she responded, her voice commendably level.

'We haven't really had a chance to . . . talk,' he said. 'How have you been?'

She essayed a light laugh. 'I told you before—I'm fine.'

'Are you?' His eyes searched her face, a small worried frown creasing a line between his brows.

Everything in her cried out to him, wanting him, loving him, but she couldn't let him know. His concern for her welfare betrayed that he was still feeling guilty for what had happened between them six months ago, but she couldn't hand him the responsibility for the empty ache in her heart. She had known what she was doing.

'You'd better be going,' she pointed out. 'They're waiting for you.'

He glanced over his shoulder. 'Oh . . . yes. Well, goodnight then, Penny. I'll see you at the wedding—maybe we'll get a chance to talk then.'

She forced a brittle smile. 'If you like,' she agreed weakly. 'Goodnight, Mike.'

'Goodnight,' he repeated. He took a step

towards her, as if he was going to kiss her, but she stepped back quickly, evading him.

'Goodnight,' she gasped breathlessly, closing the door and leaning back against it, the tears trickling slowly down her cheeks.

Oh, how she had longed for him to kiss her again—but not because he was drunk, and feeling guilty for what had happened six months ago. Those first few weeks after he had brought her back from Liverpool had been hell—every phone call, every knock on the door had shredded her nerves, as she had hoped with growing desperation that it was him.

But as time passed she had forced herself to accept that he wasn't coming. And somehow she had survived—as she would survive again. There was only one more day to get through—she could maintain her precarious façade for just that long. She'd have to try to avoid him as much as she could—if he touched her again, she would crumble into tiny little pieces.

CHAPTER TEN

'PENNY—do me a favour? Just run the iron over this shirt—it's all creased from the packing.'

'Penny, is there any grey shoe-polish?'

She smiled wryly at her reflection in the mirror. From the moment they had woken, groggy with hangovers, the two men had been in a state of near-panic. She gave up the task of tying to deal with one stray curl over her forehead that just wouldn't go into place, and went to the rescue yet again.

Chris was in the doorway of the other bedroom, one shoe in his hand. He regarded her with unrestrained approval. 'Mmm—don't you look gorgeous!'

She accepted the compliment with a smile. She was pleased with the outfit she had chosen. The colour, a glowing sapphire-blue, flattered the blue of her eyes, and the soft, silky jersey skimmed her slender figure. It had a kind of loose vest top and a pleated skirt that swirled around her knees, and a generously cut shirt to go over the top like a jacket. She wore a thin gold chain around her throat, and her mother's gold charm-bracelet on her wrist.

'Give me the shirt,' she said patiently. 'And I'll fetch the shoe-polish.'

'Thanks.' He put his arm around her waist and

gave her a quick squeeze. 'Whatever would we do without you?'

'Arrive at the church three hours late and only half dressed,' she retorted briskly, escaping from his gasp.

'Heavens, look at the time!' wailed Pete from the bathroom. 'The car'll be here any minute.'

But by some miracle, they were there on time. Most of the other guests were already assembled, the men in grey morning-suits, the women clad in every colour of the rainbow. Penny was quickly drawn into the family—they were all so friendly and welcoming that it was impossible to feel shy.

It really was a perfect day for a wedding; the sun was blazing down from a sky of purest azure blue, and there was just the gentlest puff of breeze to cool the summer heat. The church was a modern one, of red brick, with a roof like an open fan tapering to a tall steel spire, set in a wide expanse of daisy-strewn lawn.

Inside, the sun streamed through stained glass, bathing the white altar-cloth with crimson, gold and green. Penny took a seat in the second pew, just behind Pete, with Mike's sister Marion and her husband. Chris was making his interest in her blatantly obvious, swivelling in his seat to talk to her while they waited for the bride to arrive. It made her feel a little uncomfortable—she hoped no one would think she was leading him on.

Suddenly the signal came from the porch, and the rich sound of organ-music filled the church. Clare had chosen, instead of the traditional march, the music of Simon and Garfunkel's

'Bridge Over Troubled Water' and in this ultra-modern setting it was perfect.

Every head turned to catch a glimpse of the bride as she walked down the aisle, as pretty as a picture in a froth of fairy-tale crinoline. But Penny's gaze was drawn irresistibly to Mike. He was wearing a pale grey morning-suit of immaculate cut—it gave him the look of some hero from a Regency romance. He was murmuring some word of encouragement to Clare, but as he looked up he caught Penny's eye. She turned away quickly, feigning a detailed interest in the sculptured steel altar-screen.

The service began. Now it was all too easy to let her eyes wander in Mike's direction. He was standing just across the aisle from her, and a little in front so that he couldn't see her, and everyone else was watching the happy couple. It was an indulgence that wouldn't come again.

The solemn vows of the marriage service echoed in her heart. 'For better, for worse; for richer, for poorer; in sickness and in health . . .' She would always love him—maybe in time it would be something she could learn to live with, but it would always be there, etched in her heart as if scored with acid.

And then it was over, and the bride and groom, followed by the best man and the flurry of young bridesmaids, moved towards the vestry to sign the register. Suddenly Penny found that Mike was offering her his arm, all formal politeness. Pulling herself together quickly, she took it.

'You're looking a little pale,' he remarked quietly as they followed the others into the crowded vestry.

'I didn't get a lot of sleep last night,' she reminded him. 'It was nearly five o'clock when you all left.'

He smiled apologetically. 'I'm sorry.'

'Those two paid for it this morning, though,' she added breezily, detaching her hand from his arm. 'They both looked *green* when they woke up.'

'Evil woman,' put in Chris, coming to claim her. 'She's done nothing but gloat about that, ever since she came in and pulled the curtains back first thing this morning.'

Mike laughed as he moved away. 'Now that *was* cruel,' he agreed.

Chris stayed possessively at her side for the rest of the afternoon, except when his essential duties as best man forced him to leave her. She despised herself for accepting his attention, but all the time she was acutely aware of Mike, moving among his guests, and every time she sensed him close to her she found herself flirting shamelessly with Chris, just to avoid risking any contact.

Mike's house was beautiful. The original water-mill, built of golden-yellow stone, stood on the banks of a sparkling river. The new wings had been built of bricks of just the same colour, with lots of tinted glass and natural wood. A wide sweep of lawn, shaded by ancient oaks, ran along the riverside on each side of the house, and there was a narrow humpbacked bridge to the woods on the opposite bank, which were also part of the garden.

The reception was taking place, as Clare had

described, in a red and white marquee that had
been erected on the lawn, some distance from the
house. Tables laden with food stood on three
sides, and discreetly efficient waiters kept the
guests' glasses well filled with champagne as a
three-piece band played music to suit the tastes
of all from the youngest bridesmaid to the oldest
great-aunt.

As the hours passed, Penny began to feel as if
she were in a kind of bizarre dream—lack of
sleep, the unfamiliar champagne, the simmering
heat of an August afternoon were combining to
make her feel light-headed. It was becoming
increasingly difficult to cope with the turmoil of
her emotions—she had to get away.

It was growing dark. Lanterns had been lit in
the trees, their light dancing on the babbling
water of the river. Many of the children,
exhausted, were being taken off home, and the
popular music of the afternoon had given way to
a local rock band.

'What are you doing over here all by yourself?'

She glanced up as Chris came to join her on
the bridge. 'Oh . . . I just felt like a break.'

'I know,' he agreed sympathetically, slipping
his arm around her shoulders. 'It's all a bit much,
isn't it?' He bent his head, and began nibbling
lightly at the lobe of her ear. 'Do you really have
to go back to London tomorrow? Couldn't you
stay for a few more days?'

'No, I . . . really have to go,' she insisted.'

'But you'll come back, won't you? Soon? I really
want to see you again.' He drew her head back
into the crook of his arm, and his mouth closed

over hers.

She let him kiss her, wishing desperately that she could feel some response, but there was none. And as his hand began to wander close to her breast, she realised that she must finally make the position clear. She pushed him firmly away.

'I . . . I'm sorry, Chris,' she murmured. 'I like you a lot, as a person, but . . . I just don't think there's any point in taking this any further.'

The hurt in his eyes twisted the knife of guilt in her heart. 'Oh . . . But . . . I thought . . . We've had a good time, these past few days, haven't we? I won't rush you, Penny. If I've been coming on a bit too strong, I'm sorry. Just let me see you again, please.'

She shook her head. 'No. I'm sorry, it isn't your fault. It's just——'

'Is there someone in London?' he asked bleakly.

'No. There was someone. It didn't work out and . . . well, I haven't really got over it yet.'

His buoyancy was instantly restored. 'Well, if it's over! I can understand, you need a bit of time—but I'm always here, Penny. All you have to do is whistle. You know how to whistle, don't you?' he added, putting on a joking Humphrey Bogart impression.

She laughed sadly. 'Just put my lips together and blow. But don't waste time waiting around for me, Chris. I think it's going to be a long job.'

She walked away from him, and he let her go. She strolled along the riverbank, and found herself at the open french windows of the house. Several people were coming in and out, and she found herself being hailed by Marion, Mike's sister.

'Hello, Penny. Are you looking for the bathroom? It's upstairs, first on the left.'

'Oh . . . thank you,' she murmured absently.

The other woman regarded her with a friendly smile. 'Well, you've made quite a big hit with my brother,' she teased.

Penny's heart thudded, and she stared at her blankly.

Marion laughed. 'Chris! I've never known him get hooked like that. He's usually the one who does the hooking—the whole district around here is littered with the hearts he's broken.'

Penny felt her cheeks flush faintly pink. 'Oh . . . I don't really think I've hooked him,' she protested. 'He's just . . . trying to make me feel at home.'

Marion laughed, but then she was called away by one of her friends, and Penny drifted into the house.

Inside it was as beautiful as it was outside. Pale wooden floors and lots of well-tended green plants linked the modern parts with the original building, and the large expanses of glass gave it an airy feel. The furniture was mostly of Italian design, elegant but functional.

If it had been anyone else's house, she would have assumed that they had left the whole thing in the hands of an architect and an interior designer, but somehow she was certain that Mike's personal taste had played a very strong part in the construction; the firm, uncluttered, masculine lines somehow evoked his presence . . .

She had wandered away from the main part of the house, into an unlit corridor, and was gazing absently out of a window at the lively party below when she sensed that there was someone behind her. She turned sharply. 'Oh . . . It's you . . .'

Those deep hazel eyes regarded her steadily. 'Yes. I'm sorry—were you expecting my brother?'

'No.' She turned back to the window. 'As a matter of fact, I was trying to get away from him for a little while. It was getting a little . . . too involved.'

'You . . . seemed to be getting along very well with him,' he remarked diffidently.

She shrugged her slim shoulders. 'Oh, well, he's very nice, of course,' she conceded.

'Nice?'

'Yes. No more than that.' She turned to face him. 'What did you think? That we were slipping away quietly somewhere for quick grope?' she challenged, an edge of bitterness in her voice.

'I wondered.' That slightly husky voice sent a hot little shimmer along her spine. 'How have you been keeping, Penny?' he asked softly.

She met his searching gaze boldly. 'I told you, I've been fine,' she insisted, pride alone holding her head up.

'Have you?' He moved towards her, very close, and she backed away, but the wall halted her retreat. 'Then why are you crying?' He put up one hand to her cheek, and gently brushed away one single shining tear.

She stared up at him, and abruptly her defences crumbled and she reached for him, burying her face in the warmth of his chest. 'Oh,

Mike,' she whispered brokenly. 'You know why.'

He stroked one hand slowly over her hair. 'Still, lass?' he murmured, his voice unsteady. She nodded dumbly, the tears spilling over. 'Are you sure?'

She lifted her eyes to gaze mistily up into his. 'Of course I'm sure. It's never changed, not for one moment.'

'Oh, Penny.' He folded her up in his arms, burying his face in her hair. 'It's been so hard, waiting.'

'Waiting?' she repeated, puzzled.

'Six months—I made Clare wait that long, so it was only fair that I did the same.' He tried to smile. 'You're so young . . . It wouldn't have been fair to try and tie you down, just because you thought you were in love with me. I had to give you time to be sure.'

She hardly dared to breathe. 'What are you saying, Mike?' she asked tensely.

'I'm in love with you, Penny,' he said, his voice low and intense. 'I want to marry you.' He laughed, mocking himself as she stared at him, hardly able to believe what she was hearing. 'Crazy, isn't it? A kid half my age—well, nearly. I'd never have believed it was possible. But I've missed you so much, I've wanted you so much. Will you marry me, Penny?'

It was mad, crazy. She must be dreaming—or he must be drunk. But how could she be sensible, after what he had just said? She wrapped her arms around his neck, standing on tiptoe to kiss him. 'Oh, yes,' she breathed. 'Oh, of course I'll marry you.'

He kissed the tears from her eyes—tears of happiness—and then his mouth melted over hers in a deep, lingering kiss, seeking with unhurried ease all the inner sweetness. No, she couldn't be dreaming—no dream could counterfeit the warm strength of his arms around her, the growing urgency of his embrace.

He lifted his head at last, dragging a ragged breath. 'This is no good,' he murmured, those deep hazel eyes smoky with the flames of desire. 'I can't make love to you out here. Come on.'

He took her hand, and pushed open a door further along the corridor, drawing her inside and closing the door behind him. She gazed around as he flicked a switch to turn on several soft, low lights. This was his bedroom, his lair.

The bed was big—big enough to support his large frame in comfort. There was a television and stereo equipment, and a shelf of books—everything near at hand, for convenience. The colour scheme was strong—black and bronze—and the floor was covered with large rugs that made her long to kick off her shoes and wriggle her toes in the deep wool pile.

He was close behind her, and his fingers brushed lightly up her arm. 'Well?' he murmured.

She turned into his arms. 'I love you, Mike,' she whispered.

He bent his head, and her lips parted hungrily to welcome his kiss—a kiss that was almost savage in its intensity, plundering the depths of her mouth with a fierce demand that would not be denied, igniting fires inside her that would never be quenched, as long as she lived.

She curved her supple body against his hard length, moving in instinctive eroticism until he moaned against her mouth. 'I want you,' he demanded fiercely. 'I've waited six months, and I want you now.'

'Yes, Mike,' she breathed, her own need as urgent as his.

He slid his hands up beneath the fine, silky fabric of her top to find her breasts, his thumbs brushing across the tender peaks to arouse them to exquisitely sensitive buds. His mouth curved into a sensuous smile. 'You've got the most perfect breasts,' he murmured. 'Just the right size . . .'

She held his gaze with hers, deliberately provocative as she slipped the jacket of her suit back over her shoulders, and cast it aside on to a chair, and then with one smooth movement lifted the top off over her head. Her bra was a flimsy thing, almost transparent to the dusky circle of her nipples, and it fastened at the front.

He laughed, low in his throat, as he undid the clasp and let the wisp of lace fall to the floor. 'It was hardly worth you wearing that, except for giving me the pleasure of taking it off,' he chided her.

His hands were spanning her waist, and he bent his head to lap one pink nipple with his tongue. A surge of heat flooded through her, and she closed her eyes, dizzy with desire. He scooped her up in his arms, and carried her over to the bed.

There was a fevered impatience in the way they peeled off each other's clothes, a desperate need to feel the heat of flesh on naked flesh. But then their two bodies came together, quiet for a long moment, wrapped up in each other's arms.

'I love you, Penny,' he murmured caressingly.

'Mmm.' She snuggled against him. 'Say it again.'

'I love you.' He trailed his fingertips down the length of her spine, making her gasp in sheer erotic pleasure. 'I love you. And now I'm going to make love to you. Comprehensively.'

He laid her back on the bed, and his mouth claimed hers in a kiss that was a mark of total possession. She surrendered all he asked, drugged by the evocative male muskiness of his skin. His hand ran down over her body, savouring every soft curve.

She responded without reservation, thrilling to the vibrant tension of arousal in him. Their mouths broke apart as they both dragged for air, but he held her close, his kisses dusting her face, finding the tiny pulse that fluttered beneath her temple, the sensitive hollow just behind her ear.

She tipped her head back, her body moving invitingly beneath him to offer the rounded ripeness of her breasts to his devouring mouth. He made a feast of them, circling them with tantalising kisses, lapping the tender nipples with his hot, rasping tongue, nibbling erotically with his hard white teeth, suckling deeply and hungrily. Her fingers coiled into his crisp hair, holding him to her in a desperate supplication not to stop.

His hand had slid down to coax her slim thighs

slightly apart and mould over the soft, secret pleat of velvet between. His touch was exquisite, sure but gentle, his thumb tip moving rhythmically over the tiny hidden seed-pearl of sensitivity, until she was almost sobbing with pleasure.

She was melting in a warm, honeyed tide of sensuality, her whole body aroused and responsive. His magic was enthralling her; she had allowed her instincts to take over, following her heart, and she would not have believed she could be capable of such a sweet intensity of feeling.

And at last he took her, thrusting into her with a fierce male demand to which she could only surrender. She arched her body to his, moving to his wild, driving rhythm, offering herself completely to his possession. She was burning, engulfed in flame, lost in a flood of molten heat that swept through her and swept her away. He breathed her name, just once, on a shuddering sigh, and then with a last convulsive tremor he fell into her arms.

They lay for a long time just dwelling in the warm afterglow of love. And then he began to laugh, hugging her and rolling over on the bed with her, in pure happiness. 'I'm going to get a special licence,' he announced. 'We're getting married right away.'

'All right,' she agreed readily.

He stroked his hand over her cheek, suddenly serious. 'You don't mind that it has to be a register office, do you?' he asked. 'We can't be married in church, not with me being divorced.'

'Oh, Mike.' She hugged him fiercely. 'I don't

mind a bit. I'd marry you in a rowing-boat, or jumping out of an aeroplane at twenty thousand feet.'

'Well, I wasn't thinking of anything quite so eccentric,' he conceded, his eyes teasing her. 'But if that's what you want . . .'

'A register office will do me fine,' she assured him quickly. 'In fact, that's what I've always wanted—I couldn't stand a lot of fuss. But . . . What about your family? Won't they mind?'

'My mother will be furious,' he admitted blithely. 'But she's had her fair share of managing weddings for the time being—she's not going to take over ours. And as for Clare—well, she'll be delighted. She's taken it upon herself to vet every female I've been within twenty yards of these past few months, and not one has met with her approval. But she adores you.'

Penny gurgled with laughter. 'She was afraid you were going to saddle her with a wicked stepmother,' she told him.

'Was she indeed? You know, I've spoilt that girl—she's a darned sight too used to getting her own way. I feel sorry for that brother of yours.'

'Oh, I think he'll manage well enough,' she mused, slanting him a happy smile. She was so glad that he liked Pete now. 'I just hope your brother won't be too upset,' she added wryly.

'He'll just have to get used to it,' Mike asserted firmly. Suddenly he forced her back on to the bed, spreadeagling her beneath him. 'When I saw you with him at the restaurant . . .' he growled.

She quivered beneath his weight, but her eyes

met his challengingly. 'Oh? Well, it serves you right,' she declared. 'Who was that redhead you were with?'

He smiled ruefully. 'Oh, Diane's an old stand-by. She was my defence against making a complete fool of myself. I knew it was going to be hard, seeing you again, and I didn't want to risk showing my feelings until I'd had a chance to see how you reacted to me.'

'And now you're sure of me?' she asked, a small, provocative smile curving her mouth.

'Now I'm very sure of you.' His mouth claimed hers, asserting the truth of his statement. A wave of pure feminine submissiveness flooded through her, and she wrapped her arms tightly around him. But after a time he lifted his head again.

'No,' he groaned reluctantly, shaking his head as if only half convinced himself. 'We can't start making love again or we'll be here for hours. Go on, you wanton hussy, get some clothes on.' He pushed her playfully off the bed. Then he reached out and caught her wrist. 'You're staying here tonight, though,' he insisted. 'I'm not letting you out of my sight ever again.'

She danced away from him, laughing. 'You'll have to some of the time,' she pointed out. 'You've got a business to run, and I've got a lot of pictures to draw—I'm not giving that up,' she added seriously. 'It was your idea.'

He smiled. 'I wouldn't dream of asking you to give it up,' he assured her. 'There's a room downstairs, next to my study, that you can have for a studio—it's got good light, and there's not much in it but junk at the moment.'

'Oh, thank you,' she retorted sparkily. 'Are you sure you can spare me one room out of your whole big house?'

He laughed, but he took her point. 'It's your house too, now,' he said. 'Our home. If there's anything you want to change—even if you want to sell it, and start afresh——'

'Oh, no,' she responded quickly, coming back to kiss him. 'I love it. All it needs is a few flowers, instead of all that restrained greenery.'

'It shall be done,' he agreed. 'And, of course, your studio won't be the only room that'll have to be done up.' He drew her down, and kissed her nose. 'Now that Clare's moving out, her bedroom can be made over into a nursery.'

'Hey, give me time,' she protested, her cheeks faintly pink.

'All right. But not too much time,' he conceded.

He let her go, and she picked up her discarded clothes. They were a little creased, and her hair was in a wild disarray that betrayed exactly what she had been up to. Mike sat up and pulled on his trousers, watching her with warm affection as she wriggled into her underwear and fastened her skirt.

She was just pulling on her top when there was a brief rap at the door, and it opened at once. 'Mike, have you——?' Chris stepped into the room, and then stopped as he saw his brother sitting on the edge of the rumpled bed, fastening his shirt. 'Oh, sorry,' he apologised, laughing with ribald humour. 'I didn't realise . . . Penny!'

They stared at each other, he white with anger, she blushing in acute embarrassment. 'I . . . I'm sorry, Chris,' she stammered. 'I was going to——'

His eyes darkened with contempt. 'I should have known,' he sneered. 'Had your eye on the main chance all along, have you? You cheap little——'

Mike knocked him down before he could finish the sentence. He sprawled on the floor, shaking his head to clear the fog. Mike stood over him, fists clenched, waiting to strike him again, but Penny grabbed his arm. 'Mike, don't,' she pleaded urgently.

He gazed down into her eyes, and slowly his anger evaporated and he wrapped his arms around her. 'I'm sorry, lass,' he murmured. He nudged his brother with his foot. 'Get up,' he growled.

'Not if you're going to hit me again,' Chris responded promptly. 'I didn't even see that one coming.'

'I'm not going to——'

'What on earth's going on?' It was Mike's sister Marion, with her husband close behind her. She stared at her two brothers, and at Penny, open-mouthed.

'Marion?' Their mother's voice called as she, too, hurried along the corridor. 'What's the matter? We heard the most awful thump—has someone dropped something . . .? Oh!'

Penny stood there wishing the floor would open beneath her feet. It was painfully obvious to everyone what had been happening—and more relatives were crowding into the room. She tried to retreat behind Mike, but he put his arm around her, and somehow his strength seemed to communicate itself to her.

Chris looked up at them from the floor, and laughed wryly. 'It looks as if someone *did* drop something,' he remarked. 'Me—I dropped a clanger. Sorry, Mike—it was an appalling thing to say.'

Mike offered him a hand to pull himself to his feet. 'You had it wrong, little brother,' he told him. 'She was never your girl. And I saw her first—six months ago.'

'Would someone mind telling me what's going on?' came a cold voice from the door. Pete was standing there, his face set with anger. There was quite a crowd by now, but everyone else fell back staring at the two men as they confronted each other across the room.

'Certainly,' said Mike calmly. 'I'm going to marry your sister.'

The effect of his bombshell was immediate. Clare broke from Pete's arm, and threw herself across the room. '*Marry* her? Oh, that's wonderful! Oh, I'm so pleased!' She hugged them both excitedly. 'And I was so afraid you were going to marry that awful Diane creature!'

'Well!' exclaimed his mother. 'It's certainly come as a surprise. But I really am pleased.' She came forward and kissed Penny on the cheek, squeezing her hand. 'I hope you know what you're letting yourself in for,' she warned, slanting her eldest son a mischievous look. 'He can be quite the most obstinate, arrogant mule I've ever known. I've no idea where he gets it from.'

'Oh, I think Penny can cope,' murmured Mike, smiling down at her proudly. 'The first time she met me, she pulled a knife on me.'

'She did *what*?' demanded Chris, gazing at her with new respect. 'That sounds like a good story.'

'Maybe—but I'm not telling you now. I want a glass of champagne to toast my wife-to-be.'

'Another wedding,' mused his mother as they walked down the stairs. 'Well, of course, we won't have much trouble organising this one—we've had the practice. And the caterers and the florists have really done us proud—of course we'll use them again.'

'Oh, no, you won't,' Mike informed her firmly. 'We're having a nice quiet wedding—we don't want any of this fuss.'

'Oh, but——'

'No buts, Mother—or we won't invite you.'

She opened her mouth to protest, but then realised he was joking. She rolled her eyes meaningfully towards Penny. 'You see what I mean?'

Penny hugged her big man affectionately. 'Well, if your mother wants to make just a *little* fuss,' she suggested, 'we could always wait till next Saturday, and have maybe a family party . . .?'

He dropped a light kiss on the end of her nose. 'Whatever you say,' he conceded.

Chris chuckled with laughter. 'I don't think you're going to have to worry about those two,' he told his mother quietly. 'She's got him wound round her little finger!'

THIS JULY, HARLEQUIN OFFERS YOU THE PERFECT SUMMER READ!

Sunsational

**EMMA DARCY
EMMA GOLDRICK
PENNY JORDAN
CAROLE MORTIMER**

From top authors of Harlequin Presents comes HARLEQUIN SUNSATIONAL, a four-stories-in-one book with 768 pages of romantic reading.

Written by such prolific Harlequin authors as Emma Darcy, Emma Goldrick, Penny Jordan and Carole Mortimer, HARLEQUIN SUNSATIONAL is the perfect summer companion to take along to the beach, cottage, on your dream destination or just for reading at home in the warm sunshine!

Don't miss this unique reading opportunity.

Available wherever Harlequin books are sold.

Coming soon
to an easy chair near you.

FIRST CLASS is Harlequin's armchair travel plan for the incurably romantic. You'll visit a different dreamy destination every month from January through December without ever packing a bag. No jet lag, no expensive air fares and *no* lost luggage. Just First Class Harlequin Romance reading, featuring exotic settings from Tasmania to Thailand, from Egypt to Australia, and more.

FIRST CLASS romantic excursions guaranteed! Start your world tour in January. Look for the special **FIRST CLASS** destination on selected Harlequin Romance titles—there's a new one every month.

NEXT DESTINATION:
FLORENCE, ITALY

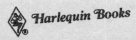

JTR7

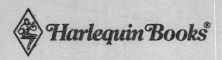 *Harlequin Books®*

GREAT NEWS...
HARLEQUIN UNVEILS NEW SHIPPING PLANS

For the convenience of customers, Harlequin has announced that Harlequin romances will now be available in stores at these convenient times each month*:

Harlequin Presents, American Romance, Historical, Intrigue:

>   May titles: April 10
>   June titles: May 8
>   July titles: June 5
>   August titles: July 10

Harlequin Romance, Superromance, Temptation, Regency Romance:

>   May titles: April 24
>   June titles: May 22
>   July titles: June 19
>   August titles: July 24

We hope this new schedule is convenient for you.

With only two trips each month to your local bookseller, you'll never miss any of your favorite authors!

*Please note: There may be slight variations in on-sale dates in your area due to differences in shipping and handling.

This August, don't miss an exclusive
two-in-one collection of earlier love stories

MAN
WITH A PAST

TRUE COLORS

by one of today's hottest
romance authors,

Jayne Ann Krentz

Now, two of Jayne Ann Krentz's most loved books are
available together in this special edition that new and
longtime fans will want to add to their bookshelves.

Let Jayne Ann Krentz capture your hearts with the love
stories, MAN WITH A PAST and TRUE COLORS.

And in October, watch for the second two-in-one
collection by Barbara Delinsky!

Available wherever Harlequin books are sold.

Back by Popular Demand

Janet Dailey
Americana

A romantic tour of America through fifty favorite Harlequin Presents® novels, each set in a different state researched by Janet and her husband, Bill. A journey of a lifetime in one cherished collection.

In June, don't miss the sultry states featured in:

Title # 9 - FLORIDA
Southern Nights
#10 - GEORGIA
Night of the Cotillion

Available wherever Harlequin books are sold.